Doctor Karmal's Machine

Surrea II

NEAL PETERSEN

Copyright © 2018 – Neal A. Petersen
All rights reserved.

No part of this book may be reproduced or transmitted or transferred in any form or by any means, graphic, electronic, mechanical, including photocopying, recording, taping or by any information storage retrieval system or device, without the permission in writing by the author.

This is a work of fiction.

Cover Design: Deirdre Wallis

Paperback-Press
an imprint of A & S Publishing
A & S Holmes, Inc.

ISBN-13: 978-1-945669-58-3

DEDICATION

Deirdre, thank you for believing in me all these years.

ACKNOWLEDGMENTS

Sharon Kizziah-Holmes and Paperback-Press, thanks for your confidence in me and my stories. Your support and expertise in the publishing process means a lot to me.

Thank you Wanda Fittro for your editing skills. I know it was a challenge but you did a great job.

Chapter One

It was a beautiful day. The birds sang cheerfully as the first of Surrea's suns rose. Like clockwork, the second sun followed exactly sixty-nine seconds after the first one cleared the horizon. The Cock'ilo crowed to signal the beginning of a new day, as everybody in the small farming town of Click was waking up. All, that is, except one.

Doctor Lucas Karmal bought the ten-acre farm, with the small three-room farmhouse and adjoining barn, to perform his time and dimensional space experiments. He stayed up the entire night making final adjustments on his machine. It had taken him four long and tedious years to perfect the mathematical formulas and finally come up with a working prototype, or at least he hoped it would work. Before he built the machine, he laboriously reviewed his formulas over and over again to make sure there were no errors possible. It had to work.

To someone watching him that morning, he would have looked like a mad scientist running around his laboratory in his white smock. His pure white hair was unkempt and ragged, quite long for a man his age. The incredibly thick glasses perched on his long, pointed nose kept slipping down to be unconsciously pushed back up with the right index finger over and over again. He worked himself into a furor, as he came closer and closer to a final product. A couple more adjustments here, an adjustment there, check his figures; recheck the countless dials, meters and scopes. Everything was perfect.

The man with the three-day-old, six o'clock shadow, stood back and looked at what he had accomplished. The rectangular machine that looked like an opaque telephone booth was finished and ready to test.

Doctor Karmal had not slept for three days. He was entirely too excited over the completion of his latest creation to be bothered by such frivolous activities as eating or sleeping. He put the supplies he prepared two weeks ago into the compartments designed for them and then took one final breath, which he held as he activated the world's first-time machine.

To his delight, the tiny fission reactor sprang into action, giving the breath of life to his master creation. The circuits came alive and all the meters and scopes seemed to be functioning properly. He turned on the closed-circuit TV and viewed his

Doctor Karmal's Machine

laboratory, possibly for the last time. The control panel had three date lines. The first one was the last date you were at, the second showed the current date, and the last one was the date you desired to travel to.

All three date lines started with the present date of 1,412,302 A.H. {after human.} He changed the last setting to a date he had always wanted to witness, O A.H., the birth of man.

He slid the power level slowly up, carefully monitoring the control board for any possible warning signals. Everything seemed to be working perfectly. The current date line was slowly moving backwards. He slid the power lever gradually up until it hit the maximum output. The present date line's first digit moved so fast he couldn't catch the numbers as they flew by.

He glanced at the current date line and watched as the year 904,72X changed before his eyes. He had already traveled over five hundred thousand years into the past in just under ten minutes. In less than twenty minutes he would be viewing what no other civilized man had ever seen, the beginning of man.

He stood glued to the monitor as he watched the breath-taking scene change over and over. Suddenly the unexpected happened. The machine shook violently like it had encountered an invisible barrier. Sparks flew inside the time machine. The good Doctor Karmal was aghast.

He didn't know what could have possibly gone wrong. He was unaware the materials he used, the metals, the plastics, even the wood was from a time completely void of magic. He had traveled back through time and his highly sensitive machine must have encountered the magical barrier, the period separating the time of magic from the time without magic. In the blink of an eye, his technological achievement changed. It lost several of its functions and gained many magical properties.

It was moving through time at a considerable speed when it hit the magical barrier. At first it didn't lose its time travel abilities, but finally it moved so far away from the time without magic that it lost this function and came to a standstill in time. It stopped so suddenly, it threw the good doctor to the ground. He hit his head and was knocked unconscious.

It was pitch black in the time machine when Lucas Karmal opened his eyes, his head hurting severely from the blow he received. He felt his scalp and found a large lump where the pain seemed to be emanating from. He groped around in the darkness, looking for the flashlight. By feeling his way around, he came to where he had it securely stored. He turned on the flashlight. Luckily, it was one of the few devices that still functioned properly. The beam of light the expensive halogen lamp produced lit the interior. Since the doctor kept his glasses on a chain, it was no problem recovering the all-important item as it dangled around his neck. He checked the current date line.

"127 803. Now why did you malfunction?" he said aloud as he checked the fission power meter. It showed zero power. He couldn't understand this. Without reinserting the control rods, it was virtually

Doctor Karmal's Machine

impossible for the nuclear reaction to cease. The meter must be broken, he thought to himself. He decided to experiment. He turned on the interior light, nothing happened. He switched on the closed-circuit TV, again nothing. Even the computer he designed was not functioning. He opened the circuit board panel and began pulling the boards out one by one and checking them. Finally, he found the problem. One of the circuit boards was burnt. He replaced it with a spare board he had the good sense to carry.

Shutting the panel, he once again checked the power meter. To his surprise, it was buried into the red. He quickly checked his other meters and scopes, only to find a disagreement between the devices. Some showed a meltdown taking place while others an absence of reaction and everything in between. He was completely perplexed by the unprecedented array of nonconforming information. He pushed the lever that caused the control rods to be pushed back into the tiny reactor, but instead of causing the meters and scopes to show reactor shutdown, the cabin suddenly filled with light. The poor doctor was very confused. Nothing inside his master creation seemed to be working properly. He noticed an extremely peculiar thing. Even though the cabin was lit, the lights themselves were off. He reached for the light switch and flipped it on. The next thing he knew, he was falling to the ground.

The machine was nowhere in sight. He sat up to see several men in armor surrounding him. One spoke in an unknown language and waved a sword. He could tell the warrior was speaking to him, but he had never encountered the crude dialect before. The doctor was a linguist and able to speak fifteen languages fluently. He said, "Friend" in all of them to no avail.

***

To the Has'ilon soldiers, the strange object that magically appeared in front of them was a possible attack against their beloved kingdom. Corporal Kitmin, being the highest rank in the small scouting party, sent one of his men back to the city to get a higher-ranking official. Something told him he didn't want to try and handle the strange problem that had fallen into his hands. He ordered the other six men in his command to make a circle around the mysterious object, until help could arrive.

Thirty minutes later an unusual thing happened. The black object disappeared and a queer little man fell to the ground in its stead.

"What is your business here wizard?" Corporal Kitman asked the frail looking man dressed in a white robe. There was no answer.

"Answer or I swear I will dispatch you back to hell with the bite of cold steel." He pointed his sword in the direction of the funny looking sorcerer. The odd little man started talking gibberish. The corporal decided to hold the man prisoner until his commander arrived. A couple of minutes later a small force came onto the scene. To Corporal Kitmins surprise, the general of Has'ilon's armies, Glamrock Clapstone himself, led the distinguished

Doctor Karmal's Machine

party. Also in the force were Glumstron Stonefoot, the Royal Advisor to the Queen and Asmond Hir'thito, the Court Sorcerer of Has'ilon and the most powerful wizard on Surrea. But, most amazing of all, the Queen, with her personal bodyguard, the dread Go'lithum, presented herself.

The seven soldiers, caught by surprise at the approach of their Queen, flopped to the ground and bowed respectfully. To everyone's surprise, so did the stranger. "Who are you?" Queen La'tian asked the funny looking man.

"My Queen, he does not seem to speak human," Corporal Kitman said.

"Asmond, communicate with him. Find out who he is and why he is here."

"Yes, my Queen." The wizard promptly threw a tongue spell, which broke down all language barriers, that is until now. "Who are you?" There was no response. "Why are you here?" Again no response. "Corporal are you sure he can speak?"

"Yes, he said several things quite clearly." The corporal tried to mimic one of the words Doctor Karmal had said.

"Friend."

"Yes friend, I mean you no harm," Doctor Karmal said in that language.

Asmond's jaw dropped. In his twelve hundred years he had walked the Surrean soil, he had never known a tongues spell to fail. Yet the stranger was completely unintelligible, the spell failing to make his words understandable. Not wanting to admit defeat so easily, Asmond tried the next logical step, telepathy. But once again, he found the impossible happened. His spell failed to penetrate the stranger's thoughts.

"What's wrong, Asmond?" the Queen asked.

"My magic does not seem to affect him. Either he is from another dimension or he is extremely powerful."

"Is there nothing you haven't tried?" she asked her confused wizard.

"Yes, but I hesitate to use a wish. It is the most powerful magic in the universe, very dangerous to use and usually has side effects."

The party considered using such a dangerous spell, but the Queen decided better of it. "Send him to a protective anti-magic cell. I will summon the wise men of the great southern kingdoms to come and try to communicate with him."

"Yes, my Queen, it shall be done," Asmond said and teleported with his prisoner to Has'ilon's prison. He arrived without the stranger and immediately returned to tell the Queen the man had escaped. But, somehow, the man was still in the same spot. Asmond began to understand what was transpiring. Either the little man was a very powerful magician or magic had no effect on him. He decided to try another spell that always worked. He threw a levitate spell on the man's frail frame, but once again, nothing happened.

The man from the future was completely unaffected by any type of magic and Asmond Hir'thito finally realized this. Only he didn't realize it included all magic, but thought it was some type of innate magic resistance.

Doctor Karmal was escorted to a prison cell. The

Doctor Karmal's Machine

wise men from the southern kingdoms were summoned and were completely stumped by their inability to communicate with the little man. Asmond finally decided to use a wish, but even this failed to produce results. Shocked by the failure of the supreme magic, it was decided to keep the man imprisoned until they could discover who or what he was and why he was here. Months went by and eventually Doctor Karmal was forgotten, left to rot in his private cell.

CHAPTER TWO

The Birth of the One-Handed Bandit of Karti'zone

Jarl Bol'itin sat with his partner Tanu Sliker in their camp, hidden from sight in the Tal'imon hills. Their three comrades had been killed in their last raid on a group of travelers, who turned out to be four mercenaries instead of the easy prey they had thought.

Even though the robbery had been successful, they were saddened at the loss of their three companions. Not because they were good friends, but because it was hard to find three good bandits to replace them. Of course, they liked the fact the bounty would be divided between just the two of them. And a good haul it was. Two hundred gold pieces and three magical items, not to mention the four magical items their associates carried.

Doctor Karmal's Machine

There were two magic shields, three rings, a sword, and a staff. The money was easy to divide, but when it came to magical items, it was a different story. There is a saying on Surrea; *nobody can trust a bandit except another bandit and he can trust him to slit his throat.*

Jarl had once been one of the most feared warriors on Surrea. He was one of Sar'garians personal guards in the second Great War between good and evil. He was the only warrior to ever fight Sterling the Great and live to tell about it. He always regretted surviving and even considered taking his own life. But, all warriors are taught from birth the only honorable way to die is on the field of honor and he held to that belief.

During the Great War, he and several other warriors were left to delay the greatest warrior in the universe. They gave a gallant fight against the great warrior and all fell in the end to his overpowering might.

Jarl was the last one standing against Sterling and bravely attacked, only to lose his sword hand during the struggle. Then he did something he has regretted for the past eleven years. He told Sterling where his master had fled, to save his own miserable life.

Since that time, he taught himself to use a sword with his left hand and became a lowly bandit robbing from the weak. Jarl knew Tanu could outfight him, but he would not let the youngster bully him. Tanu already had a magical sword, so the sword and two shields posed no problem. Jarl was happy to give up the staff for the sword, but the three rings were a different story.

"You can pick one and I'll take the other two," Tanu said with a tone of arrogance.

"I'll give you fifty gold and you pick one," Jarl countered. But, of course, this was unacceptable to either man.

"You will take sixty gold and pick one. The next time an item is found, it's yours. Get it!" Tanu demanded as he tossed the gold and a ring he didn't want at Jarl. Jarl said nothing, just frowned. He knew now was not the time. Tanu would have to sleep sooner or later; then all of it would be his. Such were the ways of bandits.

Both men acted like children playing with new toys as they donned their treasures. Jarl liked the feel of his new sword as he went through several maneuvers with it. His practice session was cut short by a loud crackle behind him. He spun around to view a black object that appeared out of nowhere.

"What is it Jarl?" Tanu asked the older, more experienced warrior.

"I don't know. I have never seen or heard of such an object."

The two bandits were cautious at first, keeping a safe distance from the strange object. They kept their guard up, not knowing what to expect. Eventually fear was replaced by curiosity and caution was thrown to the wind.

Tanu had a wand that detected magic. He pointed it at the machine and activated it. The machine radiated a glow, showing the two bandits its magical nature. Jarl jumped forward recognizing a door.

Doctor Karmal's Machine

"You said I get the next item we came across," Jarl said sarcastically, as he headed for the machine. He recklessly hopped inside.

Doctor Karmals' machine was spatially distorted, being five times larger inside than its outside dimensions. The flashlight was lying on the floor, still throwing its powerful beam against a wall. Jarl was amazed by the complexity of the control board. It had twenty-two levers, thirty-six dials and thirty-eight switches, not to mention the numerous meters and scopes.

"I've heard of a machine with enormous powers. The Argom was its name I believe, but it was described to me as a large musical instrument, nothing like this thing," Jarl said to Tanu, who was still standing outside.

Jarl's quivering hand was drawn to a lever and he slowly pushed it up. As with all artifacts or relics, one had to experiment in order to discover its powers and with all of them, there was a risk involved. Fortunately for Jarl, and by pure luck, the lever he pushed did two things. One, it turned him amoral evil and two, it gave him complete and absolute knowledge of every magical function in Doctor Karmal's, machine.

In the blink of an eye, the once great warrior became the most dangerous man in the universe. Being amoral evil, sharing was not one of his strong points, but being a loner was. He laughed hysterically. Now he could finally get revenge against the indignities he suffered due to his fight with the insignificant human known as Sterling, but first he had to squish a stickle.

***

"Jarl, is everything alright?" Tanu's voice quivered.

"Fine, just fine. So, you take advantage of a one-handed man. Leave with only your boots on or don't leave at all!" Jarl knew his tone sounded menacing and dangerous. He could have easily destroyed Tanu, but he had plans for the youngster. He wanted the world to know a new power had been born. The power of the One-Handed Bandit of Karti'zone. To justify his statement to Tanu, he melted a large boulder next to him. The young bandit turned and ran as fast as his frightened frame would move, only to find the mysterious machine appear in front of him.

He dropped to his knees and begged for mercy. "Please don't kill me Jarl, I beg you."

"Strip stickle or I will scatter your bones across the heavens." Jarl threatened the quivering youngster. Tanu did as instructed. He took off everything but his boots. Jarl turned a dial that caused a form of mind control. "Warn the world to be prepared for the One-Handed Bandit of Karti'zone! After you have told fifteen separate individuals, kill yourself. Now go."

Only two things held any form of importance in Jarl's distorted mind. First, he wanted the world to know of his supreme power, to cower to his might and to regard him as a god. Second, he wanted revenge against the so-called champion of good. He wanted Sterling to suffer like no creature ever had. A warped plan already started to form in his twisted mind, but first he had a world to defile.

***

Tanu ran from the Tal'imon Hills as fast as he could, realizing how lucky he was to be alive. There was a small farm near their camp, that used to be a hideout and he headed straight for it. His band of outlaws had purposely left the farm owners alone for two reasons. One, it was close to their camp, so if they had robbed them the chances of their hideout being found would have increased, and second, if they ever needed it for any reason, it would be handy. Tanu had really never agreed with the logic of the older and wiser members of his group, until now.

The second sun of Surrea had just dipped down below the horizon creating a spectacular sunset, when Tanu reached the small farmhouse. A lantern threw its elegant stream of light throughout the dining room. Tanu could see the Silteon family had just finished dinner when he knocked on the front door. Glont Silteon, the father of the small five-member group, got up from the table and headed for the door.

"Yes, who is it?" he yelled through the heavy wooden barrier.

"My name is Tanu Silker. I was just robbed by a bandit. He took everything I had, even my clothes. The only thing he left me were my boots." For the first time in his life, he knew how his victims felt, at least the ones he let live.

"I heard there were some bandits in the area," Glont said. He gave Tanu hospitality and clothes, fed him, and then sat down to hear the incredible tale of the One-Handed Bandit of Karti'zone. Of course, Tanu left out his connection with Jarl and changed the story to make himself out to be a lonely traveler being marauded by an extremely powerful outlaw.

"Funny I've never heard of such a powerful bandit. My brother is a castle guard in Jar'lin and tells me about any outlaws working anywhere near here."

"Oh, he just gained the machine."

"How do you know that?"

"Uh, he told me," Tanu said realizing the trap he nearly caught himself in.

"Maybe, but you can't trust an outlaw. They're notorious for lying."

Tanu didn't know why, but he felt an urge to go warn Jar'lin of the outlaw and his machine. Jar'lin was the closest kingdom around and the best place to find a new gang of bandits to join. For some reason, he kept a running count in his head of the people he told about the One-Handed Bandit. He thanked the farmer for his hospitality. It was late into the evening and the farmer invited Tanu to spend the night, but he felt an urgency to reach Jar'lin as soon as possible and turned down the offer. Tanu set off for the great kingdom, guided by the light of two of the three Surrean moons. By early morning, if all went right, Tanu would reach the great city.

Doctor Karmal's Machine

The second sun had just risen above the horizon when Tanu came over the crest of a hill to view the city before him. He had walked through the night without encountering a soul. Once he saw the city, he felt he was coming to the end of an important journey, but couldn't put a finger on why he felt that way.

He stumbled to the front gate, half in a daze. Since it was so early in the day, the streets were deserted. Only the city guards were awake and active. There were four guards at the gate and several more on the parapets above. He told the four gate guards the story of the One-Handed Bandit. One of the men hollered for the corporal of the guards and a heavy-set man came lumbering out of a building nearby. He once again told his story to the corporal who instructed Tanu to follow him. They walked through the city streets toward the King's castle near the center of the great city. By the time they reached the castle, the city streets were bustling with vivacious activity.

The corporal took Tanu straight to the countryside enforcement troop office. He bid him good day and headed back to his post. There were eleven guards in the office and one sergeant. The sergeant told Tanu to state his business. Tanu told the men his story. As he came closer to the end of his tale, he broke out in a sweat and became nervous and jittery. Finally, he reached the end and felt like a great weight had been lifted from his shoulders. He then slugged the sergeant and grabbed his sword drawing it from its sheath. The guards, shocked by his unexpected stunt, flew into action but not quickly enough. Before their startled eyes, the stranger committed suicide. The sergeant dismissed the story of a One-Handed Bandit as the delusions of a mad man and tore up the paperwork he had started, throwing it into the garbage.

Over the next couple of months, a rash of robberies and killings happened around the countryside of Jar'lin. Groups of a hundred or more travelers, peasants, and even soldiers reported the same thing; one man calling himself The One-Handed Bandit of Karti'zone, using a powerful, magical machine. Each report to the Countryside Enforcement Troop told a different ability of the strange device, but each report gave the exact same description of the object.

No matter how hard the troop tried, they could not seem to catch up with the mysterious bandit. Finally, they went to the King for help, having exhausted every other avenue open to them. The King put at their disposal every soldier in his armies and all the wise men of his council.

Normally King Tarnal would not go to this extent, but he was expecting a visit from the Queen of Has'ilon later that week and didn't want the bandit causing any problems. Since the King of Has'ilon had disappeared almost eleven years ago, if anything happened to Queen La'tian, it would leave the ten-year-old Prince Thornbolt in charge and there was no telling what the Prince might do.

For the next couple of days, the forces of Jar'lin followed lead after lead, to try and track down the One-Handed Bandit of Karti'zone without success. Even Jar'lin's most powerful wizards failed. The wise men of Jar'lin searched the archives to try and find any mention of the machine, but could not find a shred of information pertaining to the device. Finally, the day arrived when the Queen was to visit.

The King almost decided to cancel the appointment, especially since the lone bandit had increased his activities. But he didn't want his neighbors to think he couldn't handle one lone outlaw and pride intervened, so he decided to send out a large party of soldiers to escort Her Royal Highness safely into Jar'lin.

CHAPTER THREE

The Queen Does a Disappearing Act

Unbeknownst to the King, Jarl was waiting for this day. He could have initiated his masterful plan in a different way, but decided on exacting his revenge in the most warped way he could imagine. Doctor Karmal's machine had gained properties a demy-god would be jealous of. Through it, Jarl had attained a limited form of omniscience. He knew where Sterling had gone and also knew there was only one way to bring him back.

The King could have sent his entire army and it would nothave done any good. Even Go'lithum wasn't going to stop Jarl from gaining retribution for the indignations he had suffered. The time to settle the score was at hand and nothing was going to get in his way.

Doctor Karmal's Machine

Jarl waited until the queen's large group was deep into Jar'lin's territory before he enacted the first step in his plan for revenge. He knew the seventeen hundred soldiers would pose no problem. Even the Court Sorcerer Asmond Hir'thito wouldn't be a determining factor in his success. But Go'lithum was a different story. The robot from another time and dimension was possibly the only object in the universe that could destroy his machine.

None of the magic or energy the machine was capable of doing would affect the metallic monstrosity. Jarl could protect himself from the physical attacks of the robot, but his plasma energy blasts were a different story. The non-magical anti-matter energy shield the machine could produce would only handle three direct blasts in a one-minute period. Before it burned out the circuits controlling the shield. And there was no way Jarl could repair the sensitive circuitry. Since the robot never missed and was capable of a blast a second, it was a definite point to consider.

Jarl had one thing on his side. The creature called Go'lithum always had his visor down and it took nine-tenths of a second to open. Until the visor was in the open position, the robot could not attack with its energy blasts. That gave Jarl three and eight-tenths seconds to grab his victim and teleport out. Using the technology of the machine's computer, he calculated it could be done in just less than three seconds if he immobilized the magician first.

***

Has'ilon and Jar'lin bordered each other, so it was less than a day's journey by horseback from one city to the other. Rumors of a great bandit had reached Has'ilon, so a large entourage accompanied Her Highness to Jar'lin. She had her entire castle guard, her body guard Go'lithum and even Asmond Hir'thito to ensure a safe journey.

To make sure he didn't get himself into trouble, she even brought her son, feeling the seven hundred guards with her could ensure their safety against almost anything. The trip was an important one. It was time to sign a new annual trade agreement between the two sister cities.

When the royal procession reached the border, they were greeted by a thousand of Jar'lin's best troops, which put both parties' minds at ease. No outlaw, no matter how strong he was, would attack seventeen hundred soldiers. Not even the most powerful mage on the planet and the only creature to ever best Sterling the Great in battle would attempt such a feat, or at least they thought so.

As the royal party moved across the terrain, the queen wondered about such a large force meeting her at the border. Evidently the stories of the One-Handed Bandit had not been exaggerated. A force this size to escort her was unprecedented, never having more than the usual escort of around twenty of her own troops in the past. At least she wouldn't have to explain why she came with seven hundred of her own men, she thought to herself. The queen

Doctor Karmal's Machine

wondered if it had been wise to bring Prince Thornbolt on this particular journey, but then dismissed the thought. There was no way a lone outlaw would confront such a large and powerful force.

The queen was conversing with Asmond when the Elven magician she had grown to respect and admire, froze in mid-sentence with a blank look etched across his boyish features. At the same exact instant her court sorcerer became paralyzed, Go'lithum instinctively spurred into action. His only function was to protect the queen and Prince at any and all cost. The soldiers near the queen immediately knew something was amiss, when one of Jar'lin's guards yelled, "The One-Handed Bandit of Karti'zone has arrived!" Surprised and confused by the appearance of the mysterious machine, the soldiers tried to organize and repel the unexpected assault, but to no avail.

In just under three seconds from the time he appeared, the queen and the One-Handed Bandit of Karti'zone were gone. Go'lithum never got a shot off. The woman known as the most protected Queen in the universe had been kidnapped from under her guards' noses. They were dumbfounded at how quick and easy the Queen had been taken from their protection.

Both fractions separated. The King's guards returned to Jar'lin and the Prince ordered his troops to return home. Prince Thornbolt spared no time in taking his place as successor to the throne of Has'ilon. If you had asked any of the seven hundred soldiers present that day, they would have said he was more wrapped up in playing king than worrying about his mother's abduction.

The next couple of weeks marked the beginning of the fall of the Has'ilon Kingdom, as the Prince ruled the empire with an iron fist. The first thing he did upon his return was to proclaim himself King, ignoring the formalities preceding the declaration of a new king. The Royal Advisor, Glumstron Stonefoot, argued against his flagrant disregard of Has'ilon laws and to everybody's dismay, Prince Thornbolt threw him in the dungeon. The next thing the self-proclaimed King did was to threaten war on Jar'lin, if they did not find the bandit responsible for his mother's abduction and return her unharmed within three days. Of course, they didn't and the two kingdoms found themselves at war due to the whim of a ten-year-old child. Upon his declaration of war, the court sorcerer, Asmond Hir'thito and the general of Has'ilon armies, Glamrock Clapstone tried to persuade the new King to reconsider his rash decision.

"Your Highness, perhaps three days is not enough time," General Clapstone stated.

"I agree," Asmond added. "We understand the urgency of getting the Queen returned, but perhaps a measure of patience is needed."

"How dare you question my authority." King Thornbolt banged his scepter against the floor. "Guards, throw these traitors into the dungeon." The King was always accompanied by Go'lithum and because the guardian's abilities were well known, nobody dared challenge the child King. But, within the first month following the Queens kidnapping, there were two attempts on the King's life.

He held the peasants responsible and imprisoned ten more people, all of whom were innocent of the charges they were accused of. His subjects quickly grew to fear and hate their new King and he began losing control of his empire. The peasants formed an underground risistance movement in an attempt to rebel against and overthrow the tyrannical ruler. At the same time, the military made plans to release General Clapstone from captivity and then revolt against the child King.

To make matters worse, he sent the majority of Has'ilon's troops to carry out his threats against Jar'lin, leaving only a small force behind to defend the great city. An orcian kingdom discovered the child King's crass and inexperienced actions and sent an army of their own to attack the virtually undefended empire. Only one creature remained in Has'ilon with the strength and wisdom to defy the child King, the Great Omens, a powerful gold dragon Sterling himself appointed as the guardian of the castle treasury.

Omens knew only two people in the universe that could stop the seemingly inevitable downfall of the great Kingdom of Has'ilon. One was the Queen, but he knew he could not liberate her by himself. The second was not only the one warrior who could stop the downfall of Has'ilon, but also probably the only person that could rescue the Queen. The King himself, Sterling the Great.

Omens was one of the few who knew what had happened to the famed warrior. The others were the

Queen, Asmond, Glamrock, and Glumstron. Even the Prince, who never met his father, was never told of his whereabouts. Thornbolt had taken it for granted his father died in some great war long ago.

The warrior from another world had returned to his native planet nearly eleven years ago, and there was only one person capable of bringing him back to Surrea, Asmond Hir'thito. But of course, he was imprisoned, so Omens formulated a plan. He had to release Asmond and he needed to do it quickly. Has'ilon was going to fall down around the child King's head soon, very soon and Omens knew it. The fear of Go'lithum would only keep the people at bay for so long, and then even the deadly robot would not be able to repel the multitudes from killing the child King.

Dragons were known for their intelligence, wisdom, and especially their shrewd, cunning minds. Gold dragons were considered the craftiest of all. Even considering this, Omens was taking a considerable risk. The dungeon below the palace was one of the most secure prisons on Surrea. Asmond himself designed it, so Omens figured if he could get in and free Asmond, getting out would be no problem with the wizard's guidance.

Omens polymorphed himself into the guise of a human and donned the outfit of a sergeant in the dungeon guards. He also faked a royal document using one of the spare royal seals stored in the treasury. With the document in the hands of a sergeant of the guard, no one should question him. He walked into the dungeon like he owned the place, since he knew exactly where Asmond was

Doctor Karmal's Machine

being held and the layout of the prison complex. It was quite easy for him to find the correct cell. He made it through the first two sets of guards without a hitch. Since the kingdom was in a bad state of affairs, Omens didn't expect anyone to question his business. They should be more worried about their King's next commands than a prisoner escaping.

There were only two guards between him and the anti-magic cell Asmond was being held in. He approached the heavy iron bars separating him from the guards. "State your business," one of the guards said.

Omens handed him the forged document. The fake parchment stated that the prisoner Asmond Hir'thito was needed by his Royal Highness, King Thornbolt for advice in the capacity of court sorcerer concerning the war with Jar'lin. It further ordered the release of the prisoner into the custody of Sergeant Rol'igon, who was to escort him to the throne room. What Omens had feared the most happened. The guard hollered for the Corporal."Sir, we need permission to release a prisoner."

He had to act fast. The Corporal would most likely be familiar with all the sergeants in Has'ilon's dungeon guard and would immediately know he was an imposter. Omens decided to wait for the Corporal to arrive, and then if he had to, he would take all three of the dungeon guards out at the same time. He hated to have to kill three innocent people, but he knew it was the only way to save the kingdom he had sworn to defend.

The Corporal appeared on the scene and as feared he immediately noticed Omens was an imposter. To the horror of the three men, the imposter turned into his true form before their eyes. The sight of an ancient golden dragon looming menacingly in front of them, paralyzed them with absolute fear. Omens felt sorrow in his heart for what he had to do, but knew there was no other way. At least their death came swiftly as the dragon's breath engulfed them. The older a dragon became, the hotter his breath, and Omens was one of the oldest dragons on Surrea. He hoped nobody heard the sound his breath made, and luckily the guards died quietly. If someone had heard his breath, hopefully they wouldn't be able to determine the direction or what made the sound. Regardless, he had to work quickly before he was discovered. He polymorphed into a man, grabbed the cell keys off of the guard, and headed toward Asmond's cell.

***

Asmond was surprised to see the naked stranger open his cell door. In the three weeks he had been imprisoned, his only contact with the outside world had been the guard that fed him. Being a loyal soldier, he followed the rules and refused to converse with the prisoners. Thus Asmond was oblivious to the current situation of Has'ilon.

"We must hurry before we are discovered old friend," Omens said.

"Why are you risking your life for me, stranger?"

"It is I, Omens. There is not time to explain now.

Doctor Karmal's Machine

Once we are safely in the treasury I will tell you why it was necessary to free you."

Asmond stepped out of his prison and noticed the three burnt bodies down the hall. He knew Omens extremely well and realized something was terribly wrong if Omens went to the point of killing three loyal guards. Once Asmond was outside of the anti-magic barrier of his cell, it was just a simple wave of his hand to teleport himself and Omens to the treasure room. Omens explained to the impatient sorcerer what had transpired since his imprisonment. Thornbolt sending so many troops to Jar'lin, the resentment of the troops and the people, the attempts on his life and how he had dealt with it, and his use of Go'lithum as a tool of fear. He then explained his reasoning for freeing Asmond with force and how he had tried to avoid it.

Asmond was one of the wisest beings on Surrea. He felt his old friend had acted in the best interests of Has'ilon and agreed with Omens, it was time to ask King Sterling for help once again. Nearly eleven years ago, Asmond had returned Sterling to his native planet Earth and given Sterling, alias Thomas Brown, a ring with which Tom could return to Surrea if he ever wanted to. He had, however, not told Tom the ring could also be used to bring him back if Asmond ever felt it was necessary, as long as he was still wearing it. There was one drawback however. The dimensional portal between the two planets was only open for ten years every one hundred years and had recently closed. So if Asmond brought Tom to Surrea, there was no power on the planet, Asmond knew of, that could send him back to his home for another eighty-nine years.

Asmond regretted what he was doing to the earthling, but felt there was no other choice. Besides, it was his wife that had been kidnapped and the child he never met that would surely be killed if the current situation went unchanged. He drew a magical symbol on the floor and said the incantation that only he knew. As he did this he crossed his fingers and hoped Tom still wore the ring.

CHAPTER FOUR

The Return of a Legend

It had been four weeks since I made that eventful trip to Surrea. Since only a couple of earth-time hours had transpired, my life had really not changed, except for the changes within me. The several months I spent on that beautiful but deadly world would remain nothing but memories, yet I was a totally different person inside. I tried to completely forget the alter reality, the other life I had decided to leave behind.

I knew I would probably never decide to return to that wonderful planet, but I still wore the ring that would take me back if I ever wanted to go. It was sort of a trophy of my accomplishment to maintain universal harmony, Even the planet I've always known as home had supposedly been saved by my heroic deeds. If only my friends and family knew the fantastic adventures Doc and I had been through together. But, of course, if I told them they would have probably committed me. As it was, I had a hell of a time trying to explain where the numerous scars covering my body came from. I stuck to a white lie concerning a thorn bush and a blown-out tire on a friend's motorcycle.

I often wondered if Doc, my German Shepard, still had the superior intelligence he displayed on Surrea. He once told me he had always talked. I just never listened. But unfortunately, without the telepathic powers he possessed while on Surrea, he didn't seem to understand me and I surely didn't understand him. Upon our return to Earth, he became a dumb animal again, good old Doc. But even so, I owed him my life and would never forget it. I also knew he was smarter than most humans I ever met and I would go as far as to say, I truly respected him.

There was only one memory of Surrea I doubt I could ever forget. No matter how hard I tried to get La'tian out of my mind, the memory of the most beautiful woman I ever met would probably always haunt me. Even the blond bombshell who frequented the Trim and Fit Fitness Center where I worked, and had always lusted after, looked pale in comparison to the woman I had taken as my queen. It was as if my love life had been ruined and I would never find a woman who could appeal to me ever again.

I knew if I ever went back it would be because of

Doctor Karmal's Machine

La'tian. I never considered being brought back by someone on Surrea. But, if I would have thought about it, that's how I got there in the first place.

It was a beautiful day, more like a summer day than what the weather was usually like in November. Being from California originally, I was still shocked, even after fourteen years, at the inconsistency of Missouri's weather. The residents of Springfield had a saying that fit like a glove. If you don't like the weather, wait twenty-four hours and it will change. Considering I had seen it snow one day, then turn around and be eighty degrees in less than twenty-four hours, I learned when it came to the weather in Missouri, anything was possible.

I was headed to work with Doc when I had a funny feeling something was going to happen. Evidently, Doc sensed something also, because he pressed his body against mine. There was a flash of a bright white light and I found myself in my treasury in Has'ilon on Surrea. I looked at Asmond in disbelief. "Why have you brought me back?" I asked, amazed to be back on Surrean soil.

"I thought you might want to save your wife and your son's lives."

"You mean La'tian is pregnant? What's wrong, why do you need me?" My question seemed to catch him off guard then a look of understanding crossed my friend's features.

"Ah yes, I am not used to the time difference between our dimensions. Tom, you have a ten-year-old son, his name in Thornbolt. It has been nearly eleven years since you left Surrea."

Now it was my turn to be caught off guard.

Asmond explained how La'tian had been kidnapped, what the prince had done and the attempts on his life. He also told me the state Has'ilon was currently in, and Omens rescuing him from prison.

"It is time for Sterling to regain control of his kingdom and save his Queen. If there were any other way I would not have brought you back. Only you can save your son's life and rescue Queen La'tian."

As Asmond told me this, Omens brought me the four items of Omens. I was the only one in existence that could use the Ring of Omens. The sword, shield, and armor did not function without the ring. Without the four items, I was just Tom Brown, but once I donned the ring, armor and shield, and held the talking Sword of Kar'itma in my firm grasp, I once again deserved the title of Sterling the Great, King of Has'ilon, the greatest warrior in the universe. As before, I felt different inside. I possessed great power and had courage and strength I could draw on that Tom Brown didn't have. And I was once again able to converse with Doc. I was ready to conquer any obstacle.

"I'm ready to rescue my wife."

"You must be a King first and a husband second," Asmond said with his usual wisdom. Even though I knew he was right, I didn't like the idea of some bandit holding the only true love I had ever known against her will. But the needs of the many out-weighed the needs of the few and I couldn't argue against that. Besides, when I accepted the throne of Has'ilon, a great responsibility came with it. Even the son I never met had to come second; first I needed to stop a war.

"Asmond do what you can to keep my son alive. Doc, Omens, wait here till I return. I am going to Jar'lin to order my troops to return to Has'ilon," I said with the air of authority Sterling created.

Since I could teleport great distances with just a thought, it would be just a short time before I returned. Odds were, nothing would happen while I was gone. But then again, I learned a long time ago not to bet on the odds. It was a good way to lose your money.

I teleported to Jar'lin to find my army holding the great city under siege. Neither side wanted to be at war with the other, so no real skirmishes had happened yet. I knew most of my men would recognize me, so I teleported to halfway between them and the city. Sterling was known for making a great entrance and I wasn't about to change now.

I appeared with a deafening sound and a bright flash of light. My appearance prompted a low murmur from my men and the Jar'lins that rapidly built into a loud roaring cheer. The King of Has'ilon had returned. After apologizing to King Tarnal for my son's stupidity, I ordered my army to return home and quickly returned myself.

I had only been gone an hour when I reappeared in my treasury. Asmond, Omens, and Doc were not there. To my horror, the call to arms was being sounded. The city was under attack. I teleported to the front gate after drawing Sword and turning invisible. The small force my inexperienced son kept at home would be insufficient to repel the large force approaching the city from several directions.

The attacking army was too far away to determine who or what they were and where they came from. Has'ilon's only chance was Go'lithum. I once ordered the robot to attack a large enemy force in the great war between good and evil. Before I knew it, he had blasted ten thousand soldiers and the other sixty thousand scattered to escape the lethal beams of energy that killed a hundred warriors a second.

My first task was to find the metal box that was the only way to control him, and I knew exactly where it was. I teleported to the throne room, since I expected to find Go'lithum and my son Prince Thornbolt there. From what I had heard, the prince needed a good spanking and I was just the one to give it to him. But first, I needed to get past Go'lithum. Since I had fought him in the past, I knew exactly what to expect.

I was still invisible when I entered to find Go'lithum attacking Asmond who was doing his best to defend himself from the lethal blasts of energy. The self-appointed child King laughed hysterically as the robot zeroed in for the kill.

"Stop, I command you," I yelled, as I turned visible not more than ten feet from my son.

"Who dares command me to do anything?" the boy said with an insolent snarl.

"It is the true King, like I told Your Highness, he has returned." Asmond threw yet another spell to keep from being killed.

"My father is dead. How dare you let this sniveling magician talk you into impersonating him," he stated with an arrogance that astounded me. "Go'lithum kill them both!"

I didn't wait for the robots' attacks. Without a moment's hesitation I teleported behind the boy and grabbed him.

"Where's the control box, Thornbolt. The city is–" Before I could finish my statement, the ten-year-old wiggled out of my grasp and a short sword I hadn't seen in his hands came out of nowhere and bounced off my chest plate right where my heart was. If it had not been for the special armor I wore, I would have been dead. Except for the fact he was a spoiled brat, the kid was a boy any father would have been proud of. I finished the statement I started as I dodged several blasts of energy from Go'lithum.

"Has'ilon is under attack from an unknown army. At this very second they are approaching the city. Since you sent our army to attack a good friend of mine, Has'ilon is virtually undefended. Go'lithum is our only hope. Where is the metal box that controls him?" I demanded and could tell the harshness in my voice scared Thornbolt.

"You lie, the city is not being attacked; you are just trying to take away my only defense so you and Asmond can take control of my kingdom."

I could see logic wasn't working and time was growing short, so I had to use drastic measures. I tried to grab Thornbolt but he dodged my hand and brought his short sword down on my wrist. Once again my armor resisted the blow. I could tell he wasn't going to make this easy for me, so I teleported behind him and grabbed the child by his tunic.

Before he could get loose again, I teleported both of us to the front gate where the enemy was close enough to see their green skin covered by a thick orange brown hair. The Orcian army had arrived. They were still too far away to see their cat-like pupils in the middle of their yellow eyes or even their long yellow fangs that protruded from their grotesque mouth. Even from this distance, I still thought their arms and legs resembled those of an ape.

Thornbolt stood staring wide-eyed at the approaching army. He no longer resisted my hold on him. I think he realized the mistake he had made by sending so many troops and leaving the city virtually unguarded.

"Quick, where is the metal box. There is not much time."

"Are you really my father?" His tone had changed. He no longer sounded like a king, instead I heard the voice of a scared little boy.

"Yes."

"The box is under the throne, Father."

His words brought a tear to my eye; this was my son, the Prince. I was brought back to the present situation as a soldier saw his child king standing next to a figure he had not seen for many years.

The warrior shouted, "The King, it's the King." . "King Sterling has returned to save us!"

As all eyes turned to see where the soldier was pointing, a loud cheer arose and word quickly spread though the city that King Sterling had returned. But there wouldn't be a city left if I didn't get to Go'lithum quickly and send him out to defend it.

"You really are my father," Thornbolt said in disbelief and hugged me with all his might. I teleported us back to the throne room without another moment's hesitation. Go'lithum was still trying to carry out his last order, and the place was in shambles from all the energy bursts that missed their target.

"Tell him to stop." I headed for the throne, but unfortunately the prince didn't respond quick enough and one of Go'lithums' blasts caught me by surprise, knocking me a good twenty feet and dazed me. Once again, the Armor of Kim'imota saved my life from a blow that would have killed anyone else.

When my senses returned, Thornbolt was at my side with the metal box, the only device that would control the deadly robot. I looked around. Asmond and Go'lithum were nowhere in sight.

"I sent Go'lithum out to defend the city and Asmond went to help him. I'm sorry for all the trouble I have caused, Father." My son acted like a prince once again.

"Go free Glamrock, Glumstron, and the others you have jailed. I have a kingdom to save," I commanded the boy. "Thornbolt, you have made me proud. I couldn't have asked for a better son."

As I teleported to the front gate, I saw my son's face light up as a smile crossed his lips. When I materialized outside, the Orcian horde had reached the city. Go'lithum had not reached the gate yet and since he was unaffected by magic, a teleport spell would not work on him. I would just have to wait for the robot to make his way from the castle to the front gate and hope we could repel the huge army until he arrived.

My men were fighting gallantly against an overpowering force. A huge battering ram had reached the gate, but since it was protected from above and magic, my troops were unable to stop its unending barrage against the gate. Even though the front gate was reinforced and magically protected, the blows would eventually break down the barrier.

The first step was to destroy the metallic battering ram so I teleported to it. "Ah I get to see battle again. I have surely missed being used," Sword said as I brandished his superb beauty and began to kill the Orcs that were operating the thing. A swing here, a magic spell there, and the Orcs running the machinery controlling the enormous pole, were dead. Before the other Orcs could intervene, I cut the huge chain supporting the front of the pole that was slowly destroying the front gate. It fell to the ground jamming the machinery. The monstrous battering ram was now useless.

I teleported back to the parapet. Several Orcs had scaled the walls and my troops had their hands full trying to repel them as more came over the stone wall surrounding the city. Go'lithum approached the gate and I ordered him to climb the parapet and destroy the Orcian army.

Has'ilon was completely surrounded by a thirty-foot moat. There were four roads crossing the creature-infested water. Only an inexperienced leader would attack from one side, especially if he knew the city was practically undefended and I

Doctor Karmal's Machine

expected the Orcs had information to that respect.

I expected that at least two gates were under attack. I felt confident that Go'lithum could easily handle the force storming the front gate. Considering Asmond was not present, I figured he was helping hold another gate. My presence was needed elsewhere. The front gate faced north so I decided to check the east and west gates first.

I materialized in front of the east gate where there were fifty men guarding and ready for action. As soon as I appeared a soldier shouted. "It's the King!" and as one, all fifty bowed their respect. I had a very loyal and well-trained army.

"Soldier, report," I commanded the sergeant of the guard.

"All is quiet. We have observed no activity yet, Your Highness," the sergeant quickly answered.

"Keep up the good work men. Sergeant, if the enemy attacks this gate send one man to each of the other gates to find me. Is that understood?"

"Yes, my Lord, it shall be done."

Without any more hesitation, I popped to the west gate. I was just in time to see the gate being drawn open by several Orcs who had evidently breached the wall. There were about twenty of my troops still standing, but they were being overwhelmed by greater numbers. The first thing I had to do was lower that gate. A couple more feet and the city would be filled with the nearly five-foot tall, pointed-ear creatures.

Instead of killing the six Orcs that were turning the winch, it would be quicker to cut the large chain that held the gate up. Sword sliced through it like it was made of butter. The Orcs fell flat on their faces as the pressure they were pushing against suddenly disappeared. The heavy metal portcullis fell back down in place, impaling three impatient Orcs who didn't wait for the gate to be raised completely.

I teleported to the parapet to try and repel several Orcs coming over the wall. I killed five and kicked four ladders down, when help arrived. The citizens of Has'ilon, having heard the Orcs were attacking, had armed themselves with whatever they could find and came to help defend the city. I fought for another ten minutes, killing several Orcs and toppling five more ladders, until I decided my people had the situation back under control.

I checked the conditions at the final entrance into the city. Asmond was on the parapet throwing one spell after another at the horde while Omens was flying above them wreaking havoc among their ranks with his breath of fiery death. The situation seemed to be well under control. Even the soldiers and citizens who had come to help, could only stand idly by and watch, waiting to help if they were needed.

I went back to the eastern gate. The troops were still watching a deserted landscape, waiting for the invasion that never came. I went back to the front gate and as expected, the evil horde had retreated from Go'lithum's lethal blasts. He stood at the ready as if he dared them to come back within range of his deadly beams. The field in front of me was littered with thousands of dead bodies. The people's faces who were not present at the great war and seen what Go'lithum was capable of, were horror stricken by the vast carnage the robot had done in such a short time. As I stood there surveying the field, I heard several trumpets in the distance. I looked to see who made the noise and saw Has'ilon's army returning. The Orcs ran away from the superior force, disoriented and confused.

I returned to the western gate, the only one that had been overrun. Even though the Orcian forces outpowered the defenses and abilities of my people there, they had retreated, evidently warned of the return of Has'ilon's armies. The same at the rear gate. The Orcian horde had been defeated; Has'ilon was saved.

Chapter Five

Dead Men Tell No Lies

Since Has'ilon was no longer in danger and my son was once again, just a prince, thus the threat to his life ended. I turned my attention to saving the Queen, the only true love I had ever known.

"Asmond, gather Glumstron, Glamrock, and Omens together and meet me and Prince Thornbolt in the throne room."

"Yes, my lord."

I teleported to the front gate, ordered Go'lithum to return to the great hall, and teleported there myself. I appeared in the throne room to find my son in tears with Doc waiting patiently for my return.

"What's wrong, Thornbolt?"

"I found this when I returned from releasing

Glamrock and Glumstron from the dungeon." He handed me a parchment. "It was pinned to the throne with this," he added, brandishing a jeweled dagger.

Doc's thoughts entered my head. The dagger is the Queen's.

I hope you enjoyed the little army I sent your way. We have a debt to settle, you and I. Come to Hol'ikor if you want to ever see your wife alive again. The One-Handed Bandit of Karti'zone has spoken.

Just as soon as I had finished the note Asmond, Omens, Glumstron, and Glamrock entered the room. I handed Asmond the letter.

"It's good to have you back Sire. I have missed you," Glum said.

"Me feel same," Glam said in his usual broken grammar.

I was too worried about La'tian to show the appreciation I felt toward my two good friends.

"Tell me what you know about the One-Handed Bandit."

"There's not much I can tell you. He seems to have appeared out of nowhere. From what I was told, he uses an artifact of immense power that even Go'lithum could not affect with his energy beams," Asmond said.

"Maybe King Tarnal could give us some information pertaining to the outlaw and his machine," Glumstron added.

"Sire?" a soldier at the door said.

"Speak Corporal, what have you to report?" Glamrock said sternly.

"I was in charge of a scouting party a couple of months ago and we came across the same machine or should I say it appeared in front of us."

"Are you saying the wizard we imprisoned?" Asmond interjected.

"Yes, it was the same machine. I was present when the Queen was kidnapped. If anybody knows anything about that machine, it will be him."

"Thank you, soldier. Go now to duty," Glum said.

"What wizard?" I asked.

"A couple of months ago the Corporal's scouting party came across an object of unknown origin. The Corporal sent one of his men to get a higher-ranking official, evidently not wanting to handle the situation himself. The Queen, General Clapstone, Glumstron, and myself were at council when news of a strange black object appearing outside the city was reported to us.

The Queen decided to investigate the object herself against Glumstron and my advice. We accompanied her to the spot where it appeared only to find a strange little wizard. The Corporal reported the black object disappeared and the wizard fell to the ground where it had stood. Over the next several days, the wisest men in four kingdoms tried to communicate with the wizard, but everything we tried failed. Even a wish had no effect on the strange little man. The Queen decided it was best to keep him imprisoned and he has been there since. As you heard Sire, the Corporal is convinced the wizard's machine is the same one the One-Handed Bandit of Karti'zone possesses," Asmond said as

Doctor Karmal's Machine

Go'lithum entered the room.

"Has anyone asked Go'lithum if he could communicate with this wizard?"

"No, actually I never considered it," Asmond said pondering the possibility. "Fifty of the most learned men on Surrea and none of us even considered the chance of that being possible."

Also, I considered the possibility of Doc's unusual powers being able to understand the stranger's thoughts. Since Go'lithum would have to walk to the dungeon, I naturally thought it would be quicker to teleport the prisoner here, but Asmond was positive it would not work. Not that I disbelieved him, but I had to see for myself. I teleported to his guards and ordered the two warriors to take me to his cell and release him into my custody.

He was a small, older, frail-looking man. He reminded me of a science professor with his thick spectacles and white smock which was now torn and dirty. I couldn't help but feel sorry for the man who was definitely out of place in such a barbaric and dangerous world. I tried to teleport both of us back to the throne room, but as Asmond had said, I appeared by myself. I returned to the little man and motioned for him to follow me. Without any resistance, he did as I asked. We weened our way through the dungeon complex and finally returned to the throne room.

"Go'lithum do you recall this man?"

"Yes," Came the expected response.

"Did you understand the language he spoke?"

"Which one?"

The answer perplexed me. Did the stranger speak more than one language or was his language a combination of others? "Any of them."

"Yes, all but two of the fifteen he used." Now we were getting somewhere, I think.

I can read his thoughts. Doc intervened.

"Go'lithum, ask this man if he understands you, in the first language you understood that he used."

Go'lithum spoke to the stranger who lit up like a Christmas tree. He gave the robot an answer to the question.

"Go'lithum, tell me in his exact words what he said."

"Thank god somebody can speak Deltian. Yes, I understand you. My name is Doctor Lucas Karmal." Go'lithum related the man's words verbatim and Doc verified the information.

"Go'lithum, tell me in his exact words, anything he says and ask him any questions in my exact words."

"How did you get here and where did you come from?"

"I am from the future, one million, two hundred and eighty-four thousand, four hundred and ninety-nine years from now to be exact. I am from a small farming community called Click that will be built in the valley outside your city long after it is gone. I built a time machine and was traveling back to the beginning of man when it ceased to function properly, for reasons I did not have time to determine. It stopped at this time period and some very unusual things happened I could not explain or understand. The next thing I knew, it disappeared out from under me. I think it may have continued on its journey back through time. Regardless I am here and it is not." Go'lithum's metallic voice said with absolute perfection, the time traveler's exact words.

"Other than time travel, what functions did your machine have?"

"None really. Of course I don't expect you will understand this, but it had closed circuit television. This allowed someone inside the machine to see and hear what was going on outside without the use of windows or openings."

"Some fancy words for a simple clairvoyance and clairaudience ability," Asmond broke in.

Go'lithum continued. "It has a computer which is a very intelligent artificial brain. And an antimatter energy shield which acts like a simple shield, only it is invisible and would harm you if you came in contact with it. It would most likely even destroy the android I am currently conversing with. Depending on what he is made of and how he is designed. Other than that, it can create light without fire and create an electric shock that would affect anything touching the machine, and that's about it."

"Go'lithum, will the shield he mentioned affect your circuitry or harm you in any way?"

"Not enough information to determine if damage would result."

"Ask him to explain the physics behind the shield and then give me an answer as to whether you would be harmed by it or not. Ask any questions pertaining to it, until you gather enough information to make a determination."

My command resulted in a ten-minute

conversation between the two. Finally, the robot gained enough information to make a conclusion.

"I can withstand contact for an estimated one three zero point seven eight three seconds before damage results."

"Will your energy weapon penetrate it?"

"I have calculated circuits controlling anti-matter field will burn out if struck by plasma beam three times within five nine point nine five one four seconds."

Go'lithum reminded me of the Star Trek Vulcans, pure logic and non-emotional.

"Ask him if there is any way he knows of to destroy the machine."

"Why would anybody want to do that?" was Go'lithum's verbatim response.

"Doc, explain to him the situation and make him understand there might not be any other alternative."

The doctor looked around the room, trying to discover where the new voice was coming from. He looked very perplexed when he could not discover its origin.

"Who's talking to me?" Go'lithum stated.

Evidently Doc told him because he looked at him with a look of absolute disbelief on his face. A couple of seconds later Doctor Karmal started talking again.

"My God, you can communicate telepathically," Go'lithum stated as the doctor stared at Doc with his jaw hanging.

"I did not install a self-destruct mechanism within the machine, because I never considered there to be a possible need. Other than physically destroying it or the tiny fission reactor having a meltdown, I know of no way to destroy my time machine. I would like to make a request to join your excursion to find the machine, I may be of some help."

There was nothing else I could think of to ask the doctor, so I ordered his release from imprisonment and appointed two guards to make him comfortable as long as he stayed in Has'ilon. I gave him complete freedom to come and go as he pleased.

"Asmond, we're going to Jar'lin. The rest of you get prepared for a long journey and then wait here until we return."

"Am I going Father?"

"It would be best if you didn't, it will be very dangerous."

"But I am the best warrior in Has'ilon. None are my equal, that was until your return."

"The Prince speaks the truth, Sire. Go'lithum has trained him since birth in the field of warfare. The Prince beat Has'ilon's best warriors in every area during the last joust held by the Queen," Glum said. Glam supported his statement adding that he would not pick any other, besides me, to stand beside him in battle. And I must admit if it were not for my special armor, he would have killed me in the blink of an eye.

"I'll think about it," I said even though I already decided to take him. If Glum and Glam were that confident in his abilities, I would not rob my son of his chance to become a man. Besides, it would give us a chance to get to know each other, and there were still some in Has'ilon that would like to see him dead. "Asmond, lets go."

We materialized outside the front gate. The guards immediately recognized our renowned figures. Within ten minutes we were in front of King Tarnal.

"Claxle, tell me what you know of the One-Handed Bandit."

"There is not much I can tell you Sterling. He showed up a couple of months ago. Until then no one had heard of a One-Handed Bandit of Karti'zone. A Sergeant of the Countryside Enforcement Troop came to me complaining of the bandit, saying his forces were unable to track down the outlaw.

He told me a story of a man who was the first to report the bandit to their office. The man finished his story and then grabbed the Sergeant's sword and committed suicide. Since that time, this bandit has been attacking travelers, even large groups of a hundred or more, all across my kingdom. I put every resource my kingdom has to offer at the Countryside Enforcement Troops beck and call. My entire army and all my wise men could not track him down or learn of the artifact he controls. The day he kidnapped Queen La'tian was the last time we have heard of his activities in this part of the world. It's like he just vanished and went away."

"Sire, where is the man that committed suicide?" Asmond asked King Tarnac.

"He is buried at Kilt cemetery. Why wizard?"

"I have this feeling he may be able to give us more information, maybe something his id knows that his ego didn't. Call it intuition."

I took it for granted that id stood for the subconscious mind and ego stood for the conscious. "What are you planning on doing Asmond, bring him back to life and ask him?"

"No, he has been dead too long to bring him back, but his spirit can be contacted through the physical remains."

I had to make a quick decision on whether to waste the time on Asmond's hunch or not. But, at this point, we really didn't have much information pertaining to Doctor Karmal's machine. From what the doctor said and the powers reported about it, evidently the machine had changed its properties somehow. I decided to take the time to consult the stranger's remains. I told Asmond I was ready to do such. He asked King Tarnal for the use of one of his arch bishops and shortly we were at the designated grave.

Asmond turned the gravesite into mud and then raised the mortal remains of the stranger with the powers at his command. The Holy Man said a long incitation and then asked me for the first question. I looked at Asmond with a perplexed stare, being confused as to what was going on.

"You can ask him four questions, sire, but we have to be careful how we word them. The spirits don't like to be bothered and will try to trick us. The only thing on our side is the answers will be truthful and they cannot lie. However, they can give an honest but misleading answer if the question allows it."

Instead of asking do you know… we would get

two questions out of one by taking it for granted that he did know and ask him what do you know?. So, the first question we decided on was to tell us what he knew about the machine of the One-Handed Bandit of Karti'zone. His spirit told us what happened from the time it appeared in front of the two bandits until the time he had been sent to tell the world of the One-Handed Bandit of Karti'zone in explicit detail. It took an hour for the spirit to end its tale.

I asked the arch bishop to stop it when I had heard enough, but he said he couldn't without losing the other three questions. I decided to word the next question to try and exact more specific information. At least we knew his name now, although we were not sure if it was his first or last name.

"Why did Jarl kidnap the Queen of Has'ilon?"

"Probably to get revenge." Was the answer, short and sweet.

"Give the reasons for Jarl wanting revenge."
"For the several months I knew Jarl Bol'itin, all he could talk about was how he used to be one of the most feared warriors on Surrea. Jarl said he was one of Sar'garians personal bodyguards in the Great War. During the final hours of the war, he and several others were left to delay Sterling the Great. Jarl ended up being the last one left against the great warrior and valiantly attacked, only to lose his sword hand during the struggle. Then Jarl begged Sterling to kill him so he could die an honorable death, but Sterling took Jarl far away and let him live so he would suffer for the rest of his life. This

is why Jarl Bol'itin wants revenge."

I remembered the warrior he mentioned but of course, that was not what happened exactly. To the contrary, he begged me not to kill him. I let him live for telling me where Sar'garian fled to and left him where he fell to die. But Jarl Bol'itin had lived to become a lowly bandit. Now he had my wife and was using her to get back at me. For the first time since I returned to Surrea, I was scared. Scared of what this Jarl guy might do to La'tian.

There was no need to ask any more questions. I had found out what I wanted to know. It was time to return to Has'ilon.

CHAPTER SIX

The Words of Stone and Extinction

Asmond put the corpse back in the grave after the arch bishop cancelled his spell. When we left there was no evidence of us ever being there. I thanked Claxle for his help and gave the arch bishop a bag of platinum for his church. We said our goodbyes and teleported back to Has'ilon.

Glum, Glam, Omens, Doctor Karmal, Doc, and Thornbolt were waiting with Go'lithum for our return. They were all completely outfitted and ready to go. I knew I was going to have to disappoint somebody since Glum, Glam, Omens and Asmond were the only four people I knew that I felt I could trust with running Has'ilon. I didn't think the people would follow Glum or Omens and the army would not follow Asmond or Omens. Glam did not possess the knowledge or magical abilities of the others, so he was the perfect choice to stay behind. The army was already completely loyal to him, the people loved him, and he had the least to offer on the journey. I tried to be as diplomatic as possible.

"All of us gathered here today must be ready to make sacrifices for the better of Has'ilon. Omens, I need you to carry Go'lithum, Glumstron, Doctor Karmal, Doc, and Prince Thornbolt. General Clapstone you are the only one the people and the army will follow. I am putting the future of Has'ilon in your hands. You are the only logical one of the few I would trust to run Has'ilon while I am gone. I know you wanted to go on the journey before us. I wish there was someone else I trusted who I could leave behind because I could use your abilities. But, I need you here more."

I could tell Glam was hurt by my decision but, nevertheless, he took it like a true warrior and loyal subject.

"I not let you down." He held his head high trying to hide the disappointment apparent in his voice.

Before we left, I instructed the castle pages to spread the word that General Clapstone would be sitting on the throne until my return. We made a special saddle for Doc and shortly afterward our small party was flying high above Surrea headed toward Hol'ikor. I took one last look at Has'ilon as we sped toward our objective. Something told me it would be a different city when I returned, but I dismissed the thought knowing I had left Has'ilon in very capable hands.

Surrea was a beautiful planet full of life and vivid colors. Unlike earth, it wasn't cluttered with buildings, cities, and other manmade objects. It looked like what I envisioned the Garden of Eden would look like, and like Eden, it had its snake and the tree of knowledge. Only this Eden was full of snakes or evil, as it may be. It was a dangerous and deadly world. If it did have a *forbidden fruit* I had not found it yet, but I found knowledge that spanned the universe.

The thought of rescuing my wife burned into my mind to the point that I became oblivious to the beauty passing before my feet. None of us knew what to expect from Jarl. We heard the former personal guard of Sar'garian had gone mad for want of revenge against me. As everybody knows there is no telling what an insane man is capable of or is going to do next.

Omens began to tire from the extra weight he carried. Go'lithum was made of an unknown metal alloy he called steelium, even though it was lightweight, he still weighed a considerable amount. We were about halfway to Hol'ikor when we decided to rest. It was late in the afternoon and the first sun was nearing the horizon. Even if we had not stopped, it would have been late into the evening when we reached our destination, so we decided to camp and leave at first light.

Doc and Go'lithum stood guard as the rest of us bedded down for the night in our makeshift camp. The night was uneventful but, the morning was a different matter. I awoke to a woman's scream. Something seemed wrong about my surroundings but I didn't notice what was missing right off. All I could concentrate on was that scream, mainly because I recognized the voice, it was La'tian's. I hopped up and headed toward it.

I wore the leather boots I took from an ogre magi I killed before I found the Armor of Omens prior to the Great War. The magical boots gave me incredible speed, so it took no time to get where I thought her scream emanated from. At first, I thought the ring was making me see another vision like it did several times in the past, but this felt different. It was not a dream, but reality.

"My, you do respond quickly, don't you?"

I recognized the voice of Jarl Bol'itin, the One-Handed Bandit of Karti'zone. "What have you done with my wife, scumbag?"

"Your wife is of no consequence to me, she is unimportant. She will be released when we have settled our account with each other. I demand you pay a debt you owe me."

"What do you want from me Jarl Bol'itin?"

"How dare you call me by that name? Jarl was weak and a fool, he no longer exists. I am the Supreme Power, The One-Handed Bandit of Karti'zone. Soon, even the Gods themselves will fear my name. What I want from you, Sterling the Weakling, is for you to suffer as Jarl did. I owe him that much. If you ever want to see your wife again, you will do exactly what the monument of the last Great War between good and evil tells you to do."

"Where and what is this monument you speak of?"

"It is at Telk'otu bend and you above all others

should know what it is. Because of you it is there. You know I could scatter your soul across the universe right now but that would be too easy and you would not feel a thing. I want you to suffer like no other has. Go now, soon your suffering will begin."

I turned around to return to my camp and that's when I noticed what had been missing when I woke up, what had felt wrong with my surroundings. The camp was gone and so were my companions and more important, my son.

"What have you done with my friends and my son?" I yelled in agony only to be answered by an evil wicked laugh. I now had several lives to rescue. I left the area as I wanted to reach Hol'ikor as quickly as possible to find out what this madman had in store for me. As I flew through the air a thought occurred to me. Doctor Karmal and Go'lithum were both unaffected by magic of any sort. So how could Jarl have abducted them without my knowing it, unless I had been the one taken? Therefore, logic told me they were all still at the camp and I was teleported to another place that resembled it. I grabbed Sword's hilt, which connected our telepathic link.

"Sword, do you know if we were teleported while I was sleeping?"

"I have no idea, why do you ask?"

I told Sword of what had transpired in great detail. As I soared high above Surrea, I wondered if my friends and son were all right. If what I expected had happened, hopefully they would not wait long before they left the camp and would be meeting me

Doctor Karmal's Machine

at Hol'ikor. I teleported to my destination and finally realized the monument Jarl had referred to. After I severed Jarl's wrist, he told me Sar'garian was waiting at Telk'otu Bend for me. I went after him, and during the fight I shoved a fighter in between several magical spells that were cast at me. The fighter turned into stone in front of my eyes, to stand there for eternity, representing the great battle fought there that day.

I could see the large grasslands known as Hol'ikor looming before me; on the other side was Telk'otu Bend, and the spot I was to find the monument. I headed straight for it; the great expanse below me brought back memories of the courageous battle fought here. Six hundred good soldiers up against an evil horde of thirty thousand, as I fought against Sar'garian, the great evil himself, and his personal guard.

When all looked lost, an army of ten thousand Tre'tons, the living trees led by Omens, Glum, Glam, and La'tian came to join the fray turning the tide of the war in our favor. Many brave soldiers met their end at Hol'ikor, the rear battle in the last battle of the Great War. It had been almost eleven years for the beings of Surrea since the war was won but only five months ago for me. It seemed like a lifetime ago.

I reached Telk'otu Bend and drew Sword not wanting to take any chances. I landed and approached the stone warrior. At first, I wondered if I made the right decision. The statue had to be the right monument. Telk'otu Bend was deserted except for the stone fighter. That's when it moved.

"You must find the Crown of Kings and take it to the Tal'imon Hills, once you have done this, the location of Queen La'tian will be revealed to you. But first you must conquer me!" The fighter swung a sword of stone at me. The attack took me by surprise, catching me in the side, denting the Armor of Kim'imota. This was the second time since its creation that the virtually impregnable armor had been damaged. The first time by Go'lithum's fist.

I flew through the air head over heels and landed on the ground dazed and confused. Before I could regain my senses, the stone man was upon me. He swung his stone sword down on my shoulder plate, once again denting my armor and breaking the collarbone of my sword arm.

The pain brought me to my senses as he swung again. I tried to teleport, but for some reason the spell wouldn't work, so I blocked the blow with the shield of Jar'lin. Luckily, I still held Sword in my hand. The shield lost its special ability if Sword was not in my grasp. The rebound properties of my shield caused the man of stone to bounce off the ground and topple over. A flesh and blood creature's arm would have reacted to the blow, but since he was solid stone, there was no give. The warrior landed with his back to the ground, giving me a chance to regain my feet.

I slung my shield across my back and switched Sword to my left hand, ignoring the pain in my shoulder. As he stood up, I brought Sword down on his back. It barely put a notch in him and jarred my arm severely. He brought his stone shield up and caught me squarely in the midsection once again throwing me to the ground. Out of desperation, I cast a disintegrate spell at him. The spell seemed to hit some sort of field surrounding him, having no effect. Just before he reached me, I cast a force field around him.

To my horror, he just walked right through, as if it wasn't there. As a last act of defiance, I swung Sword at him. He caught it in his hand, yanked it out of my grasp, and tossed it aside. Without Sword I lost most of my powers. I felt completely helpless against the man of stone. He picked me up and threw me a good twenty feet. I hit the ground hard and was once again dazed.

The last time I felt this helpless in battle was against Go'lithum when he was under Sar'garians control. I had one last chance to beat the stone warrior. Only three of the magic spells my armor was capable of worked without Sword in my hand; an easy fall, a forceful push, and telekinesis. I doubted if forceful push would affect his enormous weight, so I used telekinesis to regain Sword. Sword flew through the air and into my grasp.

He moved rather slowly so I had enough time to try a couple of ideas. First, I tried to teleport again, but that failed. Then, I used the only way I could see out of my predicament. Since my magic didn't seem to work on him, I used it on his surroundings instead. I cast another disintegrate, but instead of throwing it at him, I cast it at the ground under his feet. A large pit instantly appeared as the ground molecules were disrupted.

The stone warrior seemed to hang in midair for a second and then plummeted to the bottom of the twenty-foot pit. Even though he had not been destroyed, I won the battle since he was unable to scale the smooth sides of his prison. As I tried to get up, I blacked out, falling back to the ground unconscious.

When I came to, it was the hottest part of the day. I felt like I was in an oven as the two Surrean suns beat down on my armor. I was covered with sweat and my mouth was so parched my tongue was swollen. I sat up, wincing from the pain all over my body, but especially in my shoulder. I noticed in amazement the stone statue stood in its original position . and the pit I created was nowhere to be found. If not for the pain I felt and the two dents in my armor, I would have thought it was all a dream.

This Jarl Bol'itin who called himself The One-Handed Bandit of Karti'zone was definitely crafty and showed a genius, however distorted it may have seemed. But the criminally insane usually displayed these traits. I wondered what his twisted mind would come up with next. I probably wouldn't have to wait very long to find out. I just hoped he wasn't so unpredictable that he would change his mind about releasing La'tian or perhaps just saying that to give me hope only to dash it in the end.

It took a lot of energy I really didn't have just to stand up. I hoped my friends were nearby because I sure could use Glum's abilities to heal right then. I teleported to Hol'ikor hoping to find them, but to no avail and once again I passed out.

I woke up lying comfortably on some pelts. It was dark and there was a large roaring fire a couple of feet from me. My wounds were healed and

Doctor Karmal's Machine

somebody had reversed the dehydration that had overcome me earlier. I was lucky my friends had found me or . . . so I thought.

"Glum, Glam, Omens, Thornbolt my son, I am lucky you found me."

"You call for those who cannot hear." A strange, crackled voice that sounded like it belonged to a hundred-year-old earthman answered. I turned around to view one of the most unusual creatures I had seen yet on Surrea. It was small, only three and a half foot tall, covered completely with purplish hair that resembled moss. I could see no hands, arms, legs, or feet. There were two stalks protruding from its top, with an eyeball attached to each. Its mouth was in the center of its body and could only be seen when it talked. Even after all the strange things I had seen on this world, I was startled by its appearance. But at the same time, the interesting being fascinated me.

"If you wish to thank someone for stopping your soul from leaving its mortal temple, that would be me. Rewop Guod, at your service." I was still not sure what sex it was, or if it even had a sex.

"What manner of race are you?"

"I am the last of my race, the last Kewa left alive and soon there will be none. We are the eldest race on Surrea, even though the Tre'tons claim such. I myself am three thousand eight hundred and..." he started counting. "Ah, yes thirty-two years old. I am the oldest living creature on Surrea. No being other than you has seen a Kewa for a thousand years.

"We used to be involved with the ways of the universe, but then a dreaded disease infected my kind. We became secluded creatures living as hermits, until the disease ran its course. I am the only one that escaped the agonizing death, caused by this incurable infliction that destroyed my race. I became so used to existing with only the gods for companions, that I remained secluded in my underground home.

"The only reason I have come out of my burrow is to help the only creature I felt deserved my attention. That is you, Thomas Franklin Brown, descendent of Sterling Justice. You have unselfishly saved all of good at the risk of your own existence and even more commendable, you succeeded where others have failed."

"Jarl Bol'itin has gained control of a device that should have never been. It must be sent back or everything that is, will cease to be. He does not realize the end result of the machine he is using. It came from a time void of magic. When it entered the magical barrier that separates the time of magic from the time without magic, it created a rift in this barrier.

The machine itself is a sponge and is slowly draining the universe of magic. Once it has attracted more magic than its molecules can hold, it will explode, destroying Surrea and sending the non-magical particles it is made of to the far reaches of the galaxy. Then these particles will once again draw the magical energy from its surroundings.

Even the atoms of our time are held together by this energy, the scientists of your world call it the strong nuclear force. Eventually, after these non-magical particles explode and then draw energy

Doctor Karmal's Machine

from the cosmos enough times, the atoms themselves will come apart destroying space itself, leaving only a void."

"As you have already realized, Doctor Karmal cannot be affected by magic, so at all costs he must be kept alive since he cannot be resurrected. If he dies, so does all of existence. This is your quest that even the gods themselves did not foresee. You must gain two items to complete this goal. First you must find the Crown of Kings, this will bring Jarl out of hiding. Since its value is priceless he will appear to claim the prize.

It is an item no outlaw can resist. Second and most important, the Mace of Turmoil must be found. However, Doctor Karmal is the only one that can touch it. Nobody else should even get near the accursed thing. If you come any closer than fifteen feet to it, a force you will not be able to resist will draw you to it. Once you are within its grip you will kill anyone to possess it, even Go'lithum would be disabled by it."

"The Mace is evil in its purest form. It is a very powerful item and has a unique ability to drain the magic out of any item it touches, making it lose its magical properties completely. If Jarl gets within fifteen feet of it he will be drawn to it, even the machine will not protect him from its powerful grasp. As soon as the Mace comes in contact with the machine, it will nullify its magical abilities and return it to the machine Doctor Karmal created originally. Jarl will have to be destroyed and the Mace returned to the machine. If the Mace leaves the machine, it will once again change and become magical. Therefore Doctor Karmal must return to his time with the Mace."

"Rewop, where will I find the Crown and the Mace?"

"The Crown is hidden deep in Deathlin's Keep and the Mace is safely protected from mortals at the Lair of the Gods. Time is growing short, go now and join your friends."

As he said these final words, night turned into day and he was gone, along with the blazing fire. I was standing in the middle of Hol'ikor in the middle of the day when something in the distant sky caught my eye. My friends and my son had arrived.

CHAPTER SEVEN

Deathlin's Keep

I was once again reunited with my friends.

"What happened to you father?"

"The One-Handed Bandit wanted a private conference with me, and did not give me a chance to argue."

"What happened, Sire?" Asmond asked. I told him what had transpired from the time we were separated till now.

"A Kewa still lives? I have not seen one since I was but a hundred years old," Asmond said. "I know where Deathlin's Keep is but I am unfamiliar with the Lair of the Gods."

"Have you heard of The Swamp of Turnos?" Omens asked Asmond.

"Yes."

"That is where the Lair of The Gods is hidden."

"That means we have to travel to the southern tip of the known world and turn around and travel to the northern tip. It is a six-month trek by foot through some of the most dangerous territory on Surrea. From the way you described the words of the Kewa we don't have much time. If it were not for Go'lithum, we could cut our adventure into smaller slices."

"What are you suggesting, Asmond?"

"Because of Go'lithum's weight, Omens cannot fly at maximum speed and must rest every six hours or so. If we went on without him we would make twice the distance in a day's time. We would save a lot of precious time, but there is still one problem. Once we reach the Mace of Turmoil we will have to stay a safe distance from Doctor Karmal, which means he will be on foot. So, I have a completely different solution. I will be back shortly, wait here for my return." Asmond disappeared.

I was famished so Glum whipped up one of his magical meals. We ate in silence as we waited for Asmond's return. Shortly after we had eaten, Asmond reappeared. He had two large carpets with him, which he unrolled.

"These are our way to the treasure."

"Don't tell me, flying carpets, right?"

"Yes, and they are the two fastest carpets I have ever seen. They used to belong to my mentor. When he gave them to me he said someday I would need them to save the world. This must be the day he referred to. If I would of thought about it, I would have grabbed them before we left. Now if

Doctor Karmal's Machine

Go'lithum and Doctor Karmal head north to the Lair of The Gods we can save a lot of precious time."

I hated to split the party up but as usual Asmond was right. I didn't feel safe leaving the universe's only hope under just Go'lithum's protection, even though he was perhaps the most powerful among us. So, I sent Omens with them and told Go'lithum to do as he commanded.

As we left them, Go'lithum climbed onto the larger carpet and gave it the command to rise as per Omen's instructions. What was transpiring had been explained to Doctor Karmal through Go'lithum's lingual abilities. I left Omens with the command to keep Doctor Karmal alive at any and all costs.

Without Go'lithum or the doctor, it was a simple task to teleport to our objective. We materialized in front of Deathlin's Keep and Glum made a remark that Horzule's Keep was a joust compared to Deathlin. Which, I guess meant it would be a much more difficult place to get through. Horzule's Keep was my first experience on Surrea, it was where I found Sword and met Glum and Glam.

The entrance was a huge skull carved out of a gigantic boulder. The skull's mouth had a large wooden double door carved to look like teeth. Asmond waved his hands, the doors swung inward, and a smell came from Deathlin's depths burning into my nostrils. A smell I had come across before. The smell of death.

Asmond spoke. "The legend is the crown used to belong to King Har'imon of the Quel'ion Kingdom. He was considered the wealthiest king of his time.

He supposedly had so much wealth he didn't know what to do with it all. He ended up buying or taking the Ten Gems of Godlihood from their respective owners and had them set in a crown of gold and platinum. It is said it took half his wealth to create The Crown of Kings. Each gem is supposed to have a powerful magical property and it is said the crown has untold powers. According to legend, whoever owns the crown can control the kingdoms of the world."

"King Har'imon had a powerful court sorcerer by the name of Deathlin Coldhand, who plotted to have the crown for himself. It is not clear how Deathlin ended up with it, no one knows for sure. He built Deathlin's Keep as a base to control the world from, but somehow, he died and so did King Har'imon, both at the same instant.

"The crown is supposed to lie at the bottom of Deathlin, guarded by unknown dangers. Several have tried to regain it but, all who have entered have never been seen again, or so I have heard. One other thing you should know Sire, before we enter the accursed place, they say the crown has a fatal curse placed upon it. Any who touch it with their bare skin and then lose it, will die a horrible death. They also say the sight of it causes greed in the purest of souls."

"We have no choice, if we do not find the crown then according to Rewop we will all die anyway. I will not force any of you to follow me or to stay on the surface. It is up to each individual whether to stay or go. Although, it might be wise for someone to stay on the surface. Do I have any takers?" I

Doctor Karmal's Machine

stood looking into each person's eyes, waiting for someone to take the out I left open and as I expected, all were silent. "It is settled then, we all go." I proceeded to lead the group into Deathlin's Keep, to an uncertain end.

The five of us stepped through the open doors into a large foyer; there were three doors on the opposite wall. The foyer was cut out of the inside of the huge skull carved boulder. Sunlight streamed in from the eye sockets and the doorway, giving it an eerie look. In front of the middle door were the remains of a forgotten warrior that had died some horrible death. All three doors looked exactly alike making me feel like a contestant on Let's Make a Deal. Only, I had a feeling, the prize would be our lives.

"My turn." Glum pulled out his magic black bag. It had been some time since I'd seen the bag I had come to associate with him. "I picked this up while you were gone Sire." He produced an oddly shaped stone, which he threw up in the air after mumbling something. The stone was shaped like an arrowhead; it fell to the ground pointing at the middle door with the skeleton in front.

"According to the Stone of Direction this is the fastest, safest way to the crown. Evidently the skeleton was placed there to try and trick you into making the wrong decision."

"The middle door it is," I said as I reached for it.

"Stop Father!" Thornbolt yelled. "It is my turn." To my surprise, Thornbolt studied the door and found a trap, a tiny needle in the handle loaded with a deadly poison. "The greatest thief in the southern kingdoms taught me his trade."

"I thought it would round out his education to be taught the reputable arts of thieving, so I hired Tark The Black to train the Prince." Glum had a huge, self-satisfied grin on his face and once again my son amazed me.

He opened the door that would have probably killed me. I drew Sword not wanting to take any more chances on walking into a trap. One of Sword's unique abilities was being able to detect any kind of trap, illusion, or ambush. The door creaked open to show a straight stairway leading down into the unknown depths of Deathlin's Keep. As soon as he opened the door, the sunlight coming in from behind us disappeared leaving us in total darkness. Somebody cast a light spell; I figured it had to be Asmond because Glum had to read his from a book to activate it. I looked at the entrance behind me only to stare at a solid wall. Our way out was gone.

I had Asmond cast another light spell on an item each of us carried just in case we became separated. Since that happened to me once before at Horzule's Keep, I wanted to be prepared. Because a light spell would not affect Sword or my armor, and my shield would rebound it, I had Asmond cast it on a dagger, which I stuck in my belt where it would be handy if I needed it.

I started down the stairway prepared to react if I had to; my four companions followed me, each being cautious in their own way. Doc and Thornbolt walked side by side just behind me, followed by Asmond, and Glum took up the rear. We walked for some time, down the seemingly never-ending stairway, when Sword stopped me.

The stairs in front of you are an illusion.

Sword caused me to see the true scene. A large ten-foot gap between the stairs became apparent. I walked up to the edge and looked down into a black void. I explained the true view to my companions. Glum said to wait a second as he once again consulted the stone. To our surprise it pointed back toward the way we had come. We turned around thinking we must have missed something. As we journeyed back up the stairs, Glum stopped and threw the stone up into the air only to have it point back toward Deathlin's depths. That meant there was something we were missing between the spot Glum was and the last spot he had used the stone.

Asmond, Glum, and Thornbolt began to search the walls, floor, and ceiling for what Asmond referred to as a secret or hidden door. Doc and I stood guard as they searched relentlessly to no avail.

"Are you sure the stone is accurate or maybe something might be influencing it?" I asked as I leaned against the wall. My hand fell upon a loose rock. I told Asmond of my discovery. Glum tossed the stone up and sure enough it pointed toward the segment of wall containing the loose rock. Asmond twisted, pulled, pushed, and then finally slid the rock up to be rewarded by a loud click. The section of wall easily opened in to show the hallway it guarded so secretly and carefully.

We continued on our mission consulting the stone as we went to try and cut down on wasted time. As soon as I entered the hallway, I felt a sense of danger, like something evil was nearby. The hallway hit a triple fork and the stone pointed to the hall on the right, which we took. We had gone about thirty feet when there was a wicked laugh that sounded like it came from behind us. Ignoring it we continued on our way. After roughly two hundred feet, the hallway ended at a metal door.

There's something following us, Doc said. *It is extremely intelligent and very evil.*

"Either we stand and fight or try to lose it, whatever it is."

No time, it's coming.

"Into the door quick," I commanded, as I took up the rear ready to confront the creature coming at us. Thornbolt searched the large metal door for any traps as the being closed in on us.

"The door's open," Thornbolt yelled as the four of them entered into its dark depths. I started to follow, but something told me I was in for the fight of my life, so I decided not to turn my back on it. I edged myself backward keeping a wary eye down the hall.

Out beyond the light I could see two red glowing eyes roughly eight feet from where I expected the floor to be. Whatever it was, it was huge.

"Don't run human, I want to play," said the most deep and wicked voice I have ever heard, followed by the same laugh we experienced earlier. I froze in my boots partially from fear and partially from curiosity. I could hear the sounds of battle behind me.

Doc do you need me?

Doctor Karmal's Machine

No, nothing we can't handle I think.

Good, because I may need your help. The creature I would call a demon entered the light. It was at least nine-foot-tall with huge bat-like wings. It had two horns next to two long pointed ears, all sticking out of its grotesque head, which was covered with a matted black mane. Its skin was red and mostly covered with black, coarse hair. The face reminded me of an Orcs but not as distorted. Its body was human, overly muscular, supported by cloven hooves, with a long arrow-tipped tail behind it. It held a flaming spear in one hand and a flail in the other.

Good guess, it is a Hollicaustian, one of the dark lord's main subjects. They live on the Seventh Plain of Hell and are very intelligent, powerful, and nasty to deal with. Be on your guard Sterling he is very tricky, Swordwarned.

I decided to try diplomacy first. One of the things I learned from Sar'garian, evil is easily scared.

"Hollicaustian, do you know me?" I said with as much authority as I could muster.

"You sound over-confident in yourself. From your question human, I gather you have done some great deed." Its voice dripped with sarcasm. "You should know me demon, I am the reason your Lord remains in his self-imposed prison. I am the Ring Wearer, the Warrior of Prophecies. I am the one to discover the Tree of Many Names, True Name, the Destroyer of Gods and the Savior of Worlds."

"Fine titles indeed, but nonetheless meaningless to me, and I doubt if you are the one that keeps my

Lord imprisoned."

"Then maybe I will tell you some of my titles you may have heard of."

"Please do, you have evoked my curiosity, but I warn you, I do not like being disappointed."

"I wear the four items of Omens…"

"I have heard of such, but still meaningless. The Destroyer of Drakstill…"

"Now you have said something I know, but alas, he was a weakling. You better top that if you want to impress me."

I narrowed my eyes and said in as deep and as wicked a voice as I could manage. "I am the Slayer of Sar'garian. I am the Greatest Warrior in the Universe. I am Sterling the Great!" I could tell my words affected the demon by the change in its expression.

"Your words have not disappointed me Sterling, if that is truly your name. If you were the one that kept my master from gaining his rightful control of the heavens, then my reward for destroying you would be unparalleled to any in the history of time. Prepare to fight Vecteron The Invincible."

"I always heard demons were intelligent, I guess you are the exception to the rule. If you wish to die, I am ready to kill." I took a battle stance.

He threw his flaming spear at me, which I blocked with my shield causing it to rebound against him and I followed with a lightning bolt. Both the spear and lightning bolt hit him causing no apparent damage as another spear appeared in his hand out of thin air.

Magic will have no effect on him, but I will.

Sword had never been wrong yet, so it looked like hand-to-hand combat was the only option left open to me. I teleported behind the demon and brought Sword down on one of its wings to be rewarded by a scream and my feet being taken out from under me by its tail. I landed on my back hard as the demon turned and shoved its flaming spear into my right shoulder plate.

Being a magical spear, it penetrated the Armor of Omens causing a searing pain in my shoulder. As soon as it hit me, it disappeared to be replaced by another one in his hand. One good blow deserves another so I took my pain out on his tail, the reason I was down. Sword sheared clean through it severing the thing from Vecteron's body. He hollered twice as loud as before, as the tail withered around on floor and black blood spewed forth from his wound.

Once again, he jabbed with his spear this time aimed at my heart. I blocked with my shield rebounding it and shoving him back. As he stumbled back, he attacked with his flail. I wondered what special properties it had. I didn't have to wait long to find out. I tried to block the weapon with my shield only to find my painful effort useless. The flail seemed to have a mind of its own, dodging my shield as the strands wrapped around my body. They constricted, drawing my arms snugly against me. I tried to teleport out of the flail's hold but found some kind of force keeping me from doing such.

So, there I was completely helpless and at the demon's pitiless control. He laughed wickedly, knowing he had beaten me, and came slowly toward me, savoring the victory he felt he had surely gained.

Quick point me at him.

Tom, we need you, came Doc's inaudible voice almost simultaneously.

Doc I'm kind of tied up right now, hang on I'll be there as soon as I can, I hope. I twisted my wrist to point Sword at the Hollicaustian's chest. I thought I knew what Sword was up to, but the demon was surely too far away.

"Now you will pay for the suffering you have caused my Master and me, Sterling the Weak."

"That's Master and I, you stupid demon," I said trying to make him mad, and it worked. He charged me leveling his spear at my chest.

Now!

As I expected, Sword increased its length like when I fought a stone giant my last time on Surrea. Instead of going from three to five feet, like it did then, it increased its length to ten, ramming right through the startled demon's chest. A look of surprise replaced the confident stare that had been across the demons' features.

Vecteron went to his knees, staring in disbelief at the gaping hole in his chest Sword left when it returned to its normal length.

Again!

Sword once again darted out catching Vecteron between the eyes penetrating the demon's brain. He made an ear-piercing scream as he dissipated before my eyes, leaving only the flail in his wake. The handle fell to the floor releasing me from its grip.

Doctor Karmal's Machine

I struggled to regain my feet. The wound in my shoulder felt like it was on fire, still burning into me. Even though I had felt his spear hit me there was no apparent damage to my armor, no hole, not even a scratch. My sword arm was completely useless; I could barely move it. I sheathed Sword, slung my shield across my back and grabbed the flail lying at my feet with my left arm. Since my right arm was useless, I rested it on my belt, holding Sword's hilt with a weak grasp. In this way, I still had my full powers and Sword's guidance.

I teleported into the room with my companions and viewed them being overpowered by another strange being. It was covered with pure white fur, like a polar bear and had the face of an ape, with one eye just above its nose. The little skin I could see, not covered with fur, was a light blue. It had large human hands and feet. Once again there were two horns protruding from its head.

Glum was standing still as if he were paralyzed. Doc was enclosed by a solid block of ice and Asmond was inside a hollow crystal rock, that looked to be shrinking in on him. Thornbolt was the only one still moving. He was dodging beams of some sort of energy, emanating from the creature's eye. I knew he would be hit sooner or later by the constant barrage of beams. Once again, my son surprised me by his adept use of acrobatic skills.

It is a cycloptic frost demon. It is nowhere near as strong or intelligent as the Hollicaustian but can be just as deadly and crafty. Be on your guard. Sword said as I teleported behind the demon.

It must have sensed my presence because it

turned as I snapped the demon's flail at it. I watched as the flail entangled the beast like it had me. The thing lost its balance and fell face first onto the stone floor after the strands forced the fur-covered legs together.

The fire in my shoulder spread through most of my body. I felt like I had a high fever. As I passed out, I saw Thornbolt leap forward and shove his short sword into the back of the demon's skull.

When I came to, I was lying on several pelts. Doc was lying with his head on my chest. I felt extremely weak. It took everything I had just to move my hand.

"You must rest, we almost lost you. If it had not been for Asmond recognizing the flail I would not have known how to treat the wound. A demon's flaming spear causes a very deadly wound, even if it is only a scratch it can be fatal if it is not treated properly," Glum said.

"Is everyone alright?" I had to fight just to get the words to form.

"Well, that's according to how you read the spell book, if you mean is everybody alive, the answer is yes."

"Don't play word games with me." I gained a little strength as anger welled up inside me.

"Asmond is trapped inside a crystal prism and you are down for a day or two, until your body recovers from the demon fire that invaded your soul."

"We do not have a day or two, is there any way to get me on my feet quicker?"

"Nothing I possess will quicken your recovery, I

have done everything I can. If Asmond was not trapped maybe he could do something I don't know."

"What is a crystal prism?"

"It would be easier to show you than try to explain it." He held up a piece of crystal the size of a walnut.

To my horror, I could see Asmond inside.

"This is one of the ways a demon traps a soul to return to hell with. Luckily for us, the cycloptic frost demon could only entrap one soul at a time. Unlucky for Asmond, he is the one the demon picked. Some of the more powerful demons can entrap as many as ten souls at a time, before having to return to hell and release them. Then they can trap more. At least that is what I have heard. As far as how to release him from it, I don't know. I have heard several things regarding a crystal prism. Like if you break it, the soul it holds is destroyed. I just don't know Sire," he said and then fell silent.

I forced my hand over to Sword's hilt and grabbed it. I explained what had transpired and asked for any information it could give.

Only three things can release the wizard from the crystal prism; the demon that imprisoned him, a wish, or a disruption spell. As far as the demon fire that infected your soul, it can be fought. You have to look deep inside yourself for the strength to overcome it. Since you are one of the few that has seen your own soul, you should be able to force the weakness from you.

I saved the universe from evil once and I was not about to let it get totally destroyed now. I had been taught by my Sensei to pull energy from within my Ki, the center of my universe or center of balance, as he called it. I called on my Ki with all my being to give me strength. I sat up in a cross-legged position normally used for meditation, but it is the best way I have found to get in touch with my Ki. I went into a trance, pulling energy to force the demon fires weakness from my soul.

When I came out of my trance the weakness was gone and Glum was trying to get me to lie down.

"Sire, if you do not rest you will never regain your strength. Lie down, I beg you."

There was a surprised look on his face when I hopped up showing no signs of the demon fires after-effects. "Fret not Glumstron, I have forced the weakness from my body. We must not tarry; we have a universe to save. Thornbolt, Doc, prepare to leave. We continue the search immediately."

"You truly are the champion of champions," Glum said. "The stone has pointed toward the wooden door. I consulted it while you were out."

The room we were in had the metal door we entered from, a door of brick, one of iron, and one of wood on each of its four walls. The wooden door was opposite the metal one. Thornbolt said he had already checked it and found no traps. I gave the flail to Thornbolt, unsheathed Sword, and opened the door.

CHAPTER EIGHT

Demons, Dragons and Platinum

I looked down a long corridor and once again felt danger; suddenly a thought occurred to me.

"Glumstron, if Dev'ilot is a cork in the top of the abyss, then how come there are demons and other nasties from the nine planes of hell walking the planet?"

"The demons we fought and even Sar'garian are but spiritual manifestations. The physical body stays on its respective plain in hell. When this spiritual image is destroyed, the demon is banished back to hell for a long period of time, before it can regain the power to once again leave its physical body and walk the face of Surrea. With Sar'garian, he was given one last chance to accomplish his mission. When you disrupted his spiritual self, his physical body was also destroyed, leaving one less lich to plague the forces of good. Of course, ten more will take his place, but such is the ways of the power struggle between the forces of good and evil."

"Is there any way to destroy a demon totally?"

"Yes, you have to kill its physical body, which means traveling into the abyss. Long ago, according to legend, ten ultra-powerful humanoids decided to try and cleanse, as a bard would say, the abyss. It is said they went in but never came out. Some say they became Kaleno's personal bodyguards. The dreaded Star Demon's."

We walked on in silence while I pondered Glum's words. The hallway seemed to stretch on forever. I was still not used to the metaphor's and sayings used by the people of Surrea, but was getting pretty good at figuring out what they meant. The words; *as a bard would say,* I took to mean, *for lack of a better word,* or *so to speak.*

"The stone says we went too far," Glum remarked after consulting the precious item.

We turned around and eventually found another secret door. Thornbolt was the one to find the hidden latch this time. We opened it to find a staircase winding down into Deathlin's dark depths. I took up the lead, as usual, ever ready to defend against any type of attack.

The stairs went down about thirty feet according to Glum who was good at determining such things. He told me once it was a dwarf's natural instinct to judge distances underground. The stairs came out at the edge of a subterranean river. A raging current

Doctor Karmal's Machine

that looked impossible to cross.

The river is an illusion, Sword revealed the true scene to me. I stared at a crevasse designed to catch the unwary traveler that was tricked into trying to cross the illusion of the raging river. The Stone of Direction pointed down a path beside the crevasse as I warned my companions of the death trap caused by the illusion.

We walked a considerable distance in the subterranean cave beside the trench. I could see just ahead of us a stone stairway going down into the rift, and somehow knew the stone would point to it. When we came beside the stairs, which only I could see, I had Glum consult the stone and sure enough it pointed straight at it. We climbed down into the gully; it was a good hundred-foot descent to the bottom. Glum used the stone, which pointed back up the stairs we had just traversed; we turned around to start back up when a voice out of the darkness halted our procession.

"Don't go, I haven't had my dinner yet this week," a deep-throated voice said. Two green, glowing eyes shone out of the darkness.

What now, I thought to myself.

It is very intelligent, crafty and wise, not to mention evil, Doc's silent voice entered my mind.

"Flattery will get you everywhere with me, little wolf." The unseen creature made the mistake of letting me know the powers of its mind. I didn't feel like playing games with the thing so I cast a force field halfway between it and my small group and then teleported to just in front of my invisible wall. The light from the small dagger shoved into my belt lit up the area around the thing. I stood looking at a dragon similar in size and appearance to Omens, except this one was black.

"Listen foul beast, I have grown tired of the insignificant beings in this dwelling. Either you can go find easier prey or I can send you back to the filthy scum infested pond you came from minus your brainless skull."

"How dare you talk to an ancient black dragon in such an insolent tone puny human? You should learn some manners from the little wolf. Beg for my forgiveness or die a slow agonizing death!"

"I guess this means you wish to die?"

"I am Thun the Terrible, I have killed over a thousand brave and mighty soldiers. Surely you have heard my name and the awesome deeds I have done?"

"No, I have never heard of you and your deeds. But maybe you have heard of my unparalleled deeds."

"Pray tell me, you have caught my interest."

"You know that is just about the same thing a Hollicaustian by the name of Vecteron said before I sent him back to hell with the bite of cold steel." The dragon's eyes narrowed when I mentioned the demon's name. I could tell Thun recognized it. "I am the champion of good, the destroyer of demons and evil gods. I am the one that annihilated Drakstill and Sar'garian. I am the strongest warrior in the universe. I am Sterling the Great! But you can just call me King Sterling, my other titles bore me," I said smugly.

As I talked, the dragon's features turned from

curiosity to fear. By the time I finished, he had backed up and I could tell he was looking for a way out of the predicament he found himself in. To put the icing on the cake I added, "Do you know a golden dragon by the name of Omens? He works for me and has enough sense to call me King Sterling. I gave you a chance to leave with your skin intact worm, now I feel like giving you a good sporting chance. I will give you a minutes head start and if you are real lucky I might not even come after you. But in case I do, you called yourself Thud the Feeble right? I want to know what to put on the plaque under your head when I mount it in my trophy room."

The ancient black dragon turned and fled as fast as his wings could carry him.

"I have never heard of a dragon running before, especially an ancient black one. They are the evilest of all dragons," Glum said with a tone of astonishment.

"If it's one thing Sar'garian taught me, it was that evil is easily scared."

"But a dragon is completely different from a lich that used to be humanoid. Both are intelligent, crafty, and wise. But most humanoids will swallow their pride, especially if they are forced to. A dragon, on the other hand, is not known for trading its pride for a horse, I'll bet a month's pay he will be back with reinforcements," Glum said sternly.

He was the only being I knew that had wisdom to rival Asmond and Omens. Once before he made a similar bet and had been correct. I doubted him then, but I wasn't going to doubt him again. We hurried back up the stairs as I began to feel an urgency to leave the huge cavern. After several tosses of the stone we found yet another secret door on the stairs against the cliff. We began searching for the hidden latch when Doc warned of the dragon's return, saying several more were with him. I cast ten force fields in a half circle around us for protection from the inevitable dragon's breath that was surely about to be used on us.

Before I could even see their eyes, a stream of black liquid came out of the darkness followed by three more. The liquid hit my invisible shield spattering against the rock walls and stairs. Wherever a drop landed steam rose as it ate into the solid rock.

I should have warned you earlier, black dragons spit acid. Oh, and one other thing, acid is the only way I can be destroyed.

How much acid does it take to harm you?

One drop and I become a regular sword, no longer the Sword of Omens.

The acid ate into the rock where it met the first force field dripping down onto the second shield. The outer shield was almost completely covered with the black acid. Then, like an air bubble, it burst. The acid, no longer having a surface to stick to, fell onto the next shield. One by one the shields disappeared until only four were left.

Will acid eat through a force field?

No, but dragons can cast spells and are probably destroying them one by one.

"Out of the way, we don't have time to find the latch," I yelled at my comrades who were

Doctor Karmal's Machine

frantically looking for the door's locking mechanism. Everybody stepped back as I cast a disintegrate spell at the rock wall. The rock dissipated to show a passageway disappearing into the darkness. "Inside quickly," I yelled as the ninth shield disappeared leaving only one between us and certain death.

As soon as we were inside, it left room for more force fields, which I wasted no time in casting just as the last barrier was destroyed. The acid that covered the last shield fell to the ground. The dragons immediately spit another round of acid at the opening of the hallway, only to be foiled by more invisible barriers.

"If I wasn't in such a hurry I would deal with you and your friends, Thud the Feeble. As it is, I cannot tarry. Maybe we will meet again and I will have more time to play," I yelled as we marched up the hall, to be answered by a cry of anguish from the dreaded beast.

"We will meet again, Sterling, you can count on that. No one speaks to an ancient black dragon as you have and lives to talk about it. I will be waiting here for your return. You better hope that whatever you seek here will protect you from my breath of death!" The rock shook from the tremendous bellow of the black dragon.

"Well, I wonder if whatever is in front of us will know we're coming. If they didn't hear you, they surely heard him."

As usual, Glum spoke words of wisdom, which I could not argue with. I led the way cautiously watching for anything looming ahead in the darkness. As we traveled along I would periodically toss a couple of force fields behind us to hinder the dragons from following us. The hallway was too small for them to traverse, but Omens had taught me the powers a dragon has. I didn't know if black dragons had the same powers as gold ones, and even Glum or Sword were not sure. Regardless I was not going to take any chances. The passage went a couple hundred feet as straight as an arrow, and then came to a silver door that was barred from our side.

"I don't like the looks of this. Nobody makes a solid silver door and leaves it lying around for no reason, and why is it barred from this side?" Thornbolt said as Glum and I looked at each other.

"Any suggestions?"

"No, nothing comes to mind," Glum answered.

I don't detect a presence anywhere, Doc said.

Silver can mean many things or nothing at all. If the Crown of Kings is behind this door, as long as you hold me I can protect you from the greed it causes. It will affect me instead, so just ignore the statements I may make. The curse is another thing entirely. I cannot protect you from that, only a Cross of Protection can. Just remember, anybody else that looks at it will do anything to possess it.

We were running out of time and the crown was not going to come to us, so there was no sense in waiting for the dragons to appear. I pulled the bar that was across the door out of its brackets after Thornbolt said it was not trapped. I began to lay it aside when Glum stopped me as he held his seven-inch-deep bag open and motioned for me to slide

Doctor Karmal's Machine

the four-foot silver bar down into its confines. I once asked him how much his magic bag would hold only to be answered with an *I don't know, I have never filled it.*

I pulled the enormously heavy silver door open. My muscles strained from the effort it took to open it with one hand. I was not about to put Sword up to open such an unusual door without knowing what was behind it. Glum seeing the tremendous effort I had to apply, came to my aid. With his help, the door swung open quickly, without a sound.

I looked into the barren room. My light, filled the space, and I was blinded by the refection, as the torchlight increased tenfold. As soon as my eyes adjusted, I stared in amazement at the solid silver walls, ceiling, and floor. I started to enter the room when Sword stopped me.

The room is filled with several traps; half the floor is covered with them.

I noticed there did not seem to be any doors or openings out of the room, just solid silver walls. "Glum, consult the stone again."

"Yes Sire." He tossed it into the air. It pointed into the room.

"What's wrong?" Glum asked evidently noticing the worried look on my face.

"The room is covered with traps."

"Since I do not see any exits, I would bet at least one of them takes us to where we want to go or opens a portal or something of that nature," Thornbolt stated. I agreed it was a logical guess. Glum said the stone would lead us to the correct trap, if a trap were indeed an exit.

Sword, can you tell me where the traps are, to the point I can safely traverse the room?

I can try. I didn't like Sword's answer but what choice did I have? Behind us was certain death and if we gave up, our death would be forthcoming, so into the room it was.

A ten-foot square in front of the door is trapped. On all three sides of the first trap are ten-foot squares that are clear.

After warning everybody, I teleported us to the clear area directly in front of where we were standing. Just in case the stone bounced or Glum threw it at an angle toward a trap, I cast a force field around us to make sure a trap was not set off accidentally. Glum tossed the stone up twice, I asked him why.

"First, I asked it to point to the safest and quickest route to the crown and second, I asked it to point to the trap that allowed us to continue our journey. At any rate as you can see it pointed the same direction both times." As the stone pointed to our left. Sword described more of the room. From his description of the trapped areas and the clear ones, the eighty-foot room was beginning to look like a chessboard.

I dispelled my force field and teleported us twenty feet to the center of the next safe square. We followed the same procedure as before. I cast a protective force field, Glum consulted the stone twice, and we teleported to the next clear area the stone pointed to. After several times of going through this process we completely circled a square the stone kept pointing at. I started to step onto the trap when Glum stopped me.

"Wait!" he yelled. "We must all step onto the trap together," he insisted.

"Why?" I asked as Doc warned of the dragon's approach.

"I cannot tell you how I know, let's just say I had a vision."

I learned a long time ago to trust Glum's wisdom and insight and I wasn't going to change now. I teleported us all together over ten foot to the center of the trapped area. The instant we teleported three things happened. First, a small stream of black liquid came from the hall, flying through the air right where we had just stood. The dragons had caught up with us. Second, a large silver door appeared on the wall twenty-five feet in front of us. And third, the floor disappeared leaving only a ten by thirty-foot strip from us to the door that had just appeared.

"Quick follow me!" I ran toward the door casting a force field behind us for protection from the dragon's attacks.

"It's a good thing you had that vision Glum." I glanced down into the black void below, and saw the dragon breath that just barely missed us.

I hit the latch and threw my body into the heavy silver door, while, at the same time, I cast another barrier. Because of my increased strength, resulting from a flow of adrenalin coursing through my body, the door flew open like it was light as a feather. As soon as I opened it, the floor behind us reappeared. And hopefully the traps as well, I thought.

We charged through the door. As soon as we

cleared it, I began casting one force field after another, until I had placed fifty barriers between us and the unknown number of dragons dogging our trail.

"That should slow them up for a while," I said after I placed the last barrier. Just to make sure we were headed in the right direction, Glum consulted the stone once again. To our relief, it pointed down the hallway. I could only imagine how long and difficult our search would have been without the Stone of Direction to guide us.

As we walked down the hall, a bright flash of light mixed with an agonizing scream came from behind us. *I guess the traps did reappear with the floor,* I thought heartlessly, as an evil grin crossed my lips.

We continued on our way down the hundred-foot hallway, turned a corner, and stood in front of another silver door. Glum's eyes lit up.

"That's not silver, it's platinum," he said with an unmistakable tone of greed. His eyes grew glassy with a blank stare, evidently calculating the possible worth of the object. Surrea's monetary system is built on minerals, gems, and sellable items. Copper is equal to an American dollar, silver a five-dollar bill, gold a ten spot and platinum, the rarest of minerals on the planet, is worth a hundred. Gems can be from a worthless stone, to a stone worth a million platinum pieces.

Dwarfs are naturally greedy, valuing minerals and gems above all else; they are the planet's gem experts. A full-blooded dwarf can tell you the worth of a gem at a glance, and Glum was no exception.

Doctor Karmal's Machine

We were here for one reason and one reason alone. "Glum." I said only to be ignored. "Glum!" I hollered bringing him out of his spell of greed.

"Yes Sire?"

"Use the stone to check the proper direction" I said, a little angry with him for ignoring me.

"Yes, My Lord," he mumbled and tossed the stone up. It fell pointing at the door.

"Through the door it is." Once again, I began to pull yet another door open, after Thornbolt checked it for any possible traps. I had to strain but not near as hard as I did with the silver door.

Being the one in the doorway, I was the first to look inside, as my light filtered into the recesses of the dark room. In the center of the solid platinum room was a platinum pedestal with the Crown of Kings resting squarely on it.

"Nobody look into the room, that is an order!" I commanded. The room was barren except for the platinum pedestal and four pillars encircling it, each at least a good ten feet away.

It has powers beyond comprehension and is worth more than anything else on the planet. We would be a fool to give it up, take it for ourselves! Sword was raving hysterically.

"I wish I had a cross of protection," I muttered.

Don't worry about that. Once we have it, no one would dare try to take it from us. We must have it!

"Here take mine," Thornbolt said. "Mother gave it to me when I turned seven."

I grabbed the cross and placed it around my neck while Sword tried to convince me to grab the sacred item. I was now completely protected from the crown's negative effects.

There, now you don't have to fear the curse. Take it, it is ours, I want it, I want it now! Sword said wildly, building itself into a frenzy.

Sword? No answer, *Sword?*

Yes, what do you want? It to come to you? What are you waiting for? Go get it!

Sword! If I die trying to gain it, then you won't possess it.

It's worth dying for!

Yes, but it is even worth more to live for and possess its powers. I attempted reasoning with Sword.

That's true. Then what are you waiting for? Go get it.

I'll make you a deal. You help me gain it, and I will get it for you. O.K?

Yes, yes, anything, just get the crown.

Are there any traps between it and us?

Yes, three, now that you mention it. There is also some type of field in a five-foot radius around it, in the shape of a dome.

"Glum hand me a dagger or something you don't need."

"Here Sire," Glum held a dagger over his right shoulder.

I threw it at the invisible shield, as hard as I could. The dagger ricocheted off the barrier, bounced off a wall and skidded a good forty feet. As soon as it hit the floor a large ball of flame erupted. It went another ten feet and ten steel spears came shooting out of the thirty-foot high ceiling with such velocity they stuck into the platinum

Doctor Karmal's Machine

floor. Another twenty feet and there was a bright flash of light and no more dagger.

The barrier is gone and I don't detect any more traps. They seem to all have been deactivated. There is nothing between us and the crown. Go get it quick!

I tried to use a telekinesis spell on it, but nothing happened. I didn't quite trust Sword, so I had Glum give me two more daggers. The first one I tossed at the invisible barrier. It skimmed over the top of the crown hitting the opposite wall. The shield was gone. I slid the second dagger across the floor. Nothing happened, so I told Glum to hand me a pelt and his magic bag.

I stepped into the room and headed straight for the crown. It was truly magnificent. It had nine of the ten stones still mounted securely in it, one had probably fallen out long ago. The stones were enormous in size, at least as large as a thirty-karat diamond each, some maybe larger. Each stone was a different color, one was a bright baby blue, another a deep rich green. There was a dull dark purple, an orange, a solid white, and a light pink stone. Another was a deep red, the most priceless ruby I had ever seen, and next to it, a sparkling flawless diamond. But the one that caught my eye was a black diamond that seemed to have infinite depth within its rich confines.

The Ten Gems of Godlihood, each one worth a King's ransom. The only diamonds of their kind in existence.

What about the ruby and the emerald? I asked sword. *I am not even sure what the rest are?* I was totally transfixed by the beauty of the rare and precious stones.

They are all flawless diamonds, perfect in every aspect.

That is a diamond? I thought as I pointed in amazement at the red stone. *I would have sworn it was a ruby.*

Yes, and all ten are present. The Diamond of Gol'nita is invisible and perhaps the most powerful of the ten. The legend of the Gems of Godlihood is that before the God Kaleno was banished to the abyss by the father of the God's, Kalena, he fell in love with Astrial'i, the most beautiful God of all. He made the twelve gems of Godlihood with the power his father granted him and gave them to her trying to buy her love. When Kalena sent Kaleno to the bottom of the abyss, Astrial'i threw the gems away out of anger and to repent the love she had nearly given the evil one. The gems fell to Surrea and were scattered across the known world. So far only ten have been found and it is said that if the other two, the brown diamond of Sol'tarn and the yellow diamond of Hark'imont, are ever found and put with the ten in the crown, the owner would gain the power to control the universe.

I finally broke my bewildered and awestruck stare. I covered the Crown of Kings with the animal pelt I held.

Sword continued explaining the legend. *It is believed by many that Kaleno possess the two missing gems and has been trying to gain control of the other ten. Some say Kaleno influenced King Har'imond to make the crown, thus gathering the ten gems together. Then he tricked Deathlin into taking it, to bring to him, but somehow Deathlin broke the spell. Some believe the spell was broken though the power of the crown. It is said the curse killed the King, and Kaleno killed Deathlin at the same instant by coincidence. Deathlin built this place through the power of the crown and hid it so well, none have ever found it, until now. Supposedly Kaleno has had his servants searching Deathlin's Keep for centuries trying to find the crown. If he ever gains all twelve stones, he will be able to destroy Dev'ilot, thus releasing him from his imprisonment.*

We had accomplished what no other being had been able to do in the history of Deathlin's Keep, I picked up the Crown of Kings and began to stick it in Glum's magic bag. There was a loud bang behind me. I twirled to see what made the noise, and realized the platinum door had slammed shut.

I should have realized there was more of a reason why the crown had not been taken from Deathlin for so many years, even though thousands had looked for it. We found it too easily. Asmond said it was guarded by unknown dangers. Well I sure had been fooled.

I teleported to the other side of the door, but reappeared on this side of it. Evidently, I was unable to leave the room until the door opened on its own or something to that effect. Out of the corner of my eye I thought I saw something move. I turned to see what it was. I looked straight at one of the four pillars, and as I stared in horror, the pillar transformed into a platinum warrior.

I quickly looked at the other three pillars and to my dismay they also had turned into metal fighters.

Oh great, one stone warrior nearly killed me, and now I have four metal ones to deal with. I tied Glum's magic bag to my belt, then I tried to disintegrate the floor below the closest platinum man. The floor disappeared and so did the metal warrior. There was a bright flash and fire leapt up from the hole just after the platinum fighter disappeared into its depths.

Well at least my disintegrate works. The other three creatures converged on me. *This is going to be easy.* Two of the metallic men were close enough together to get with one spell. Since I only had five disintegrates in one day's time, I wanted to use them sparingly. I had already used two today and I didn't know if I would need one later.

You only have one disintegrate left! Sword hollered, but too late. I cast my last one at the two metal men's feet. Once again, as soon as they disappeared from sight, there was a flash of light followed by fire.

What do you mean that was my last one? I've only used three since we entered Deathlin, haven't I?

Yes, but you used two against the stone statue earlier today.

That was today? I thought that was yesterday.

Well at least my odds were better, I only had one creature to deal with now. I considered the spells I had left. I could make myself invisible to anything in the material plane, by going to the ethereal plane and hope it couldn't reach into that existence, but that would not destroy the thing. I doubted if an ice storm, fireball, slow, or lightning bolt would affect it. That left a forceful push or telekinesis and I knew it would weigh too much for those to do any good., And that was the extent of my offensive spells.

Your assumptions are correct, none of your attack spells will affect it. You're going to have to find another way to destroy it.

I'm just going to have to use my strongest weapon against it, my brain.

I studied the platinum warrior as it approached me, it moved slow and sluggish. There had to be a way to destroy it without fighting it hand to hand. A plan began to formulate in my head.

I cast a fly spell and flew up to the ceiling out of the warrior's reach. I turned invisible and immediately cast an intangible image directly in front of me. I then directed my image down to the edge of one of the holes I had made in the floor. Unfortunately, it didn't take the bait, which meant I was going to have to be the bait.

I flew down to the floor and hovered above one of the holes, in the center of it, out of his reach. As I had hoped, the thing lumbered up to the edge of the hole and took a swipe at me to test the distance. I teleported behind it with my shield ready. It turned around slowly and took a swing at me with its hand. The attack was slow and easy to block. His hand hit the shield and rebounded, throwing the thing off balance. I put the tip of Sword against its body and gave it a little push. The creature fell back into the hole.

I watched it fall and then burst into flames; I had

won.

The door opened on its own. I was free. I walked out of the room only to be hit by a hundred questions from my companions.

"I will explain later, right now we need to get out of here," I said, stifling the incessant questions being thrown at me.

Getting in had been extremely difficult, but getting out was a completely different story. We easily ascended and were once again on the surface of Surrea. I just wished for Asmond's sake we would have known where the crown was hidden so we could have just teleported to it.

The next stop was to get Asmond released from his prison, and then on to find Omens, Go'lithum, and Doctor Karmal. All in all, the crown had been fairly easy to obtain. I just hoped the rest of my mission would be as simple. Something told me it wouldn't be.

CHAPTER NINE

Legends, God's, and a Temple

It was well past midnight when we materialized outside Deathlin's Keep. As I looked at the entrance to the underground complex it slowly vanished, leaving a solid boulder to mark the spot. I guess the Crown's power was all that kept the evil place in existence. Once the Crown of the Kings had been removed, Deathlin's Keep was no more. I wondered what happened to the creatures that still lurked in its depths, like the black dragons. I guess I would never know.

The first thing I wanted to do was free Asmond. Since we could all use a good night's sleep, I decided to go to Has'ilon. We materialized in the throne room. Most of Has'ilon was asleep at this hour. The dead hour's guard (as they called them on

Surrea) were just about the only ones stirring in the castle and deserted streets. Since we didn't want to disturb anybody, we quietly retired to our respective rooms. Sword assured me Asmond would be fine until tomorrow, so I decided to release him first thing in the morning.

I had Doc stay in the Royal Chambers with me, to insure no one would try to take the crown. Even though nobody but us knew it was in my possession, I was not about to take any chances. The night was uneventful. I awoke feeling renewed and refreshed, ready to continue with the quest that had befallen me.

The first thing on the agenda was getting Asmond released, so I teleported Doc and I to the Silver Hand, Has'ilon's wizard's guild. One of Asmond's duties as the court sorcerer of Has'ilon, was being the guild master. Whenever Asmond was gone, the second most powerful mage in my kingdom, Til Norn, took his place. Til was human and nearly ninety years old. You wouldn't expect a man who looked like he belonged in a convalescent home to be capable of such power and destruction. But this was not the good old Terra Firma back on earth. It was Surrea and if there was one thing I had learned on this strange and unusual planet, it was to not be surprised by anything and to expect the unexpected.

The elder mage opened the huge door leading into the lone tower known as the Silver Hand of Has'ilon. "Your Highness, I was not expecting you back for quite some time. How may I help you?"

"I need your assistance, Til." I entered the sacred

building where only magicians were allowed. But since I was the King, I had been made an honorary member, even though I didn't know how to do things a simple apprentice could perform. I brought out the crystal prism and showed it to him. "Asmond had an accidental run in with a demon who thought he would make a nice addition to hell. Are you capable of casting a disruption spell?"

"Yes, my lord. Place the crystal on the floor and stand back."

I did as instructed and watched as the adept magician proved his title of being the second most powerful mage in Has'ilon. The spell he cast caused the crystal to shatter. A white smoke rose from its confines forming the outline of a humanoid. The mist solidified and Asmond's physical body once again walked the surface of Surrea.

"It is good to have you back old friend."

"Where are we? What happened?" Asmond was evidently dazed and confused by the ordeal he had been through. I explained the events of the day before as he collected his wits. By the time I finished, Asmond was his old self again and we were ready to continue on our quest.

We teleported back to the castle, after giving our respects to Til. Thornbolt and Glum were waiting for us, ready to go. Other than Til and a guard or two, I hadn't seen a soul since our return. I took a final look at my throne room. I had the same queer feeling I felt two days ago when I left Has'ilon, but as before, I dismissed the thought. The strange feeling had been wrong then and it had no reason to be considered now.

We teleported to the designated meeting place outside the Swamp of Turnos. Asmond figured it would be eighteen or nineteen days before Doctor Karmal, Omens, and Go'lithum reached the Tree of Dissolution, where we had decided to meet.

The Tree of Dissolution was just as dead and hideous as the Tree of Many Names was alive and beautiful. The Tree of Many Names, whose true name was the Tree of Souls, contained every color imaginable, compared to the Tree of Dissolution's black charred remains.

As I stood comparing the foul monstrosity before me to the unforgettable memory I had of the Tree of Souls, the most breathtaking sight I had seen on Surrea so far, I asked Asmond where it received its name.

"I really could not tell you Sire, its legend has never been told to me. Maybe Omens would know." For the first time since I had known the elven magician, he couldn't answer one of my questions. Other than not knowing where the Lair of the God's was, he always knew or at least had an answer.

My curiosity was starting to get peaked about such an unusual name, so I asked Omens.

"Long ago, a great kingdom used to be here. The King was a very powerful ogre by the name of Turnos. It is said this tree was the most beautiful thing on Surrea and the source of his power and strength. His reign lasted for six hundred years and all the kingdoms around feared his might.

"Their fear became so great they joined together to destroy the kingdom of ogres. The other kingdoms devised a plan to cause King Turnos' demise. They discovered a poison rumored to be so deadly one drop would kill the strongest thing alive. Even creatures resistant to poison would be affected by the lethal liquid. The formula was discovered in an ancient book of alchemy in one of the kingdom's archives. The rulers of these other kingdoms spent a considerable amount of money to gather the ingredients together, some of which were very rare and very hard to acquire. It took six months from its discovery to have the deadly poison in their possession. At first, they tried to poison Turnos, but that didn't have any affect.

"They were astonished. Especially since they had already tested it out on some prisoners that were to be executed. They knew the assassination didn't fail because of the poison. Something had to be protecting the ogre King. One of the wise men learned that the Tree of Beauty, which is what this tree was called then, was the source of his power and protection, and if the tree was destroyed the kingdom would fall."

"It is said the sage was tricked into believing this information came from his own god, but as it turned out, Kaleno was the power behind the destruction of Turnos. In the end the kings were unknowingly beguiled by Kaleno into hating the ogre King and tricked into poisoning the Tree of Beauty. The most beautiful object in the universe withered away and died along with the Orle'ak Kingdom. King Turnos cursed the world with his last breath, Orle'ak turned into a swamp, and the Tree of Beauty became known as the Tree of Dissolution because nothing will grow near it. Because of this, ogres and humanoids have been at war since, and the world lost its most beautiful prized possession."

"I heard that ogres and humanoids used to live in peace, but never knew why they hated each other so much," Asmond commented.

Glum had his arms crossed on his chest, with a disgusted look on his face, showing his defiance toward the statement. "I find it hard to believe dwarves and ogres ever lived in peace."

Seeing Glum's mood change drastically, I decided to move on to another subject. "Does anybody know the story behind the Mace of Turmoil and the Lair of the Gods?"

Glum's mood once again changed and he was able to add his knowledge to the conversation, "I can tell you about the mace, but not the lair."

"Please do, I am all ears."

"I would be happy to Sire, but what do you mean *I am all ears*?"

"It is just a figure of speech on my planet, it means I am listening. Please continue."

"Oh, you mean to say, *you are the singer*," Asmond interjected.

I guess since Bards were the story tellers on Surrea, and the way they told their stories was to sing them, I could see the reason for the saying.

Glum took a deep breath. "Anyway, a hundred lifetimes ago a great dwarven king named Glimstoll Hammerhand acquired enough wealth to make anybody and everybody consider conquering Akenshield, a very powerful kingdom. His brother Axestoll Hammerhand was greedy even by dwarven standards and plotted to overthrow his good brother.

Doctor Karmal's Machine

He hired an evil magician to make a mace to his specifications.

"But, unbeknownst to him, the evil wizard cross plotted him. Being a follower of Kaleno, he asked the great evil to put the most powerful of curses on the magical mace and make him immune to the curse. As you know, this curse caused anything that came within fifteen feet of it to become platinum mad, killing anything foolish enough to get in the way of it possessing the mace."

"The sorcerer gave the mace to Axestoll and teleported him to Akenshield's throne room before Axestoll realized what the mage was doing. Over the span of three days the dwarven kingdom all but annihilated itself. The wizard's army walked right in and destroyed the remaining inhabitants of Akenshield. The magician ordered his troops to stay clear of the southern end of the kingdom where the mace was located, but his plans went astray when an eight-year-old child found the mace and moved it to the center of the kingdom. Before the mage realized it, his troops were fighting amongst themselves as he searched the southern end in vain. By the time he discovered what happened to the mace, what was left of his entire army was fighting to gain control of it. When it was all over, the magician was the only living creature left. He became known as the wizard with the sardonic garrison and later the name was shortened to Sar'garian. As far as the mace goes, it became known as the Mace of Turmoil. It disappeared and was never heard of again."

"I can finish the story where Glumstron has

stopped singing."

Turning toward the golden dragon, I listened intently. "Please do."

"After the destruction of Akenshield and the invading army, the gods understood the destructive power of what the mortals referred to as the Mace of Turmoil. They decided it was too dangerous to leave lying around and realized it had to be hidden from the creatures of Surrea. Since it could only be destroyed by being tossed into the fires of hell, and the gods themselves would be affected by its irresistible force, they had to devise a way to conceal it from the curiosity seeker and the ignorant.

"The gods thought carefully about what to do with the perilous item. Finally, they decided to hide it where very few ventured, the Swamp of Turnos was such a place. Then they felt it needed more protection than just an untraveled swamp, so they created the Lair of the Gods. What this lair is and what may be lurking inside it, no one knows for sure. None have attempted to recover the mace as far as recorded history shows. If any have ventured into its unknown confines, they have not returned to tell about it."

We spent the rest of the evening discussing past wars and events. I listened intently to all the tales and legends being discussed that night. They told of great deeds and evil ones, the fall of empires and the birth of great kingdoms, even fables concerning the gods and their all-powerful might. I fell asleep listening to the fantastic deeds of some long dead wizard.

Doctor Karmal's Machine

I awoke to find myself standing before the Gods of Space and Time. Since I had been before the galaxies that called themselves this once before, I immediately recognized their majestic forms.

Once you came to us for help mortal. One of the beings lit up letting me know which one was addressing me.

Now we have brought you before us. I noticed another one light up, which was helpful since they all sounded the same to me.

It is time for you to repay the debt you have incurred for our help. A third one lit up.

The relic from the future is a danger none can ignore, even us. Therefore, we have decided to help you succeed in your endeavor. Since no magic can affect the man from the future, existence must wait for him to catch up with time... I was not sure what the God meant by this.

Even though we cannot affect him, we can however affect the object of his arrival to the Swamp of Turnos. At his present speed, by the time the quest was finished, life would cease to exist. Therefore, his speed must be increased to a point that is not so fast it would kill the man from the future, but fast enough to save eternity. This is a fine point because time is running out for all of existence. When you return to the one planet that contains the true evil, you will be with the man of importance. Protect him from any and all harm. The true evil will try and stop you if he discovers the truth about the machine. He would rather perish with all of existence than live another day in his prison. As of yet he does not realize what is transpiring. We have kept him from gaining this knowledge.

He has learned that you entered Deathlin's Keep, but does not realize you have gained the Crown of Kings yet. If he learns the crown has once again been recovered from its hiding place, not only will you have to deal with the machine, but you will also have to deal with the great evil's armies. He will stop at nothing to gain the ten Gems of Godlihood encased in the crown. Once he has all twelve gems in his possession, he will once again walk the heavens. He only has one gem in his possession and with the ten in the crown he would only have to gain the last one to escape his ageless prison. This must not happen.

We are giving you the knowledge of how to find the Lair of the Gods and how to enter it. Even though this will aid you, it will still be a very dangerous task.

Inside the lair is Thagoreum, a creature placed there eons ago. A spell of absolute power was put on him so even the gods could not move him from his task of keeping any and all from removing the mace from his protection. He must be destroyed before the mace can be won. He cannot be harmed by physical or magical means. Even Go'lithum or the Sword of Kar'itma will not harm him.

For the first time since I first encountered the supreme entities, the last god spoke to me. His voice was different than the rest and reached deep into my soul. I felt more insignificant than I could have ever dreamed possible. Even the other gods seemed trivial compared to him. For the first time since I had been told his name, I heard the words of Kalena.

You have made me proud my son. But now you face the hardest and most important task you have ever tried to accomplish. Thagoreum is the most powerful being on Surrea, I myself created him. The only way to defeat him is through the powers of your mind. You must use the Crown of the Kings to accomplish this. Whatever happens, do not let loose of your grasp on the Sword of Kar'itma or all will be lost. Do not get within twenty feet of the Mace of Turmoil because nothing can protect you from its curse. It will take you and the animal you call Doc to defeat Thagoreum. Only the two of you should enter the lair, but remember Doc cannot look at the crown. Doc has powers of the mind he does not yet comprehend and is the only one of any and all beings that can destroy Thagoreum in the present existence. If he finds the power within himself to destroy the behemoth, then the mace will be yours for the taking. The mace and crown must be taken to the Tal'imon hills by Lucas Karmal and placed together. The future is in the hands of mortals, it is in your hands, Thomas Franklin Brown.

The next thing I knew, I was standing on the flying carpet next to Doctor Karmal.

"Quick, Omens, Go'lithum, climb on." But before either of them could follow my instructions, the carpet took off like a rocket. "Meet us at Jar'lin," I yelled as they quickly disappeared from sight. I didn't know if they heard me for sure and I wondered how Go'lithum would respond to an order he could not carry out.

It seemed like we were constantly picking up speed, the countryside flew by so rapidly it got to a point where we had to lie down to keep from being pushed off the accelerating carpet by the forces it was pushing against. I could tell the G-force was beginning to affect Doctor Karmal, whereas, my armor protected me from experiencing the same.

I grabbed hold of him while hanging onto the edge of the carpet with my other hand. We traveled through the night and into the daylight hours. The good doctor slept while I hung onto him, not daring to let myself fall asleep.

A couple hours after dawn the carpet began to slow and within a couple of minutes it was back to its normal speed. In the distance I could see the Swamp of Turnos with the Tree of Dissolution standing like a lone sentinel, guarding the entrance to a place just as bleak and barren as the tree itself. I still found it hard to believe something so twisted and grotesque could have once been so beautiful and astounding.

I could see my friends standing under the hulking monstrosity. They looked like ants milling around some huge insect waiting for it to fall. The carpet landed in the camp upon my command.

"How did you manage this?" I could tell by his expression, Asmond was totally perplexed. "We thought you went to sleep, but the next thing we knew, you were gone. We woke up this morning and you were still missing, I was beginning to get worried that maybe the bandit had gotten hold of you or something. The next thing I know, you show up with Doctor Karmal, and your hair has turned

Doctor Karmal's Machine

totally gray. I'm confused. Where are Omens and Go'lithum?"

I explained what happened and my experience of meeting the father of all creation. I felt I could not put into words how I had been touched by the Supreme Being. How it had changed me, how it had pierced my soul, like I had been stuck with a red-hot razor-sharp blade.

Even though I was extremely tired, we started into the swamp. Nothing grew between the tree and the boundaries of the quagmire. I felt an urgency to reach the Lair of the Gods, like I was being drawn to it. I began to imagine what Thagoreum might look like. What kind of beast it may be that Kalena referred to as the most powerful creature on Surrea. My thoughts were interrupted by Doc.

There is something in front and behind us.

"Doc, Asmond, Glum, protect Doctor Karmal as all costs! Thornbolt, get whatever it is behind us, I will take the front."

It is some type of reptile; no intelligence and I can't communicate with it.

I didn't feel like waiting for it to come to me so I ran through the tall weeds that grew everywhere in this swampy wasteland. Ten feet from where I had stood, I came across the creature that blocked our path. It was a reptile alright, but slightly larger than the average garden variety– a lizard twice the size of a large alligator.

Luckily, I had long ago got into the habit of holding Sword's hilt, since it could not communicate with me if I didn't. And as always, Sword was a wealth of information. *It is a basilisk, it breathes fire and its gaze will turn you to stone. Do not look into its eyes.*

I immediately looked away from it. How could I fight something I couldn't even look at? Maybe it would be better to just immobilize it and go around the thing, then kill it.

Use your shield as a mirror. Its gaze will not affect you from a reflection.

Good advice, I thought, as I heard the swamp lizard lumbering toward me. I tilted my shield to where I could see the reptile and cast a force field around it. One down, one to go, I thought as I teleported back to my friends.

"What is it?" Asmond asked me as I materialized in front of him.

"A basilisk. Where is Thornbolt?"

Asmond pointed in the direction of the second beast. "He went after the other one."

"I hope he knows what he is dealing with." I quickly ran after him. To my horror, I came across my son froze for eternity in solid stone. I heard a hiss to my left and swung my shield into place, leveling it so I could see the creature.

Partially out of anger and partially out of frustration, I cast a disintegrate spell at the giant lizard. I watched as its molecules dissipated and felt gratified in knowing I had destroyed my son's killer.

"Asmond, Glumstron, come quickly!" I yelled, fighting the sorrow trying to overcome me at the loss of a son I barely knew, but still loved greatly. How would I face his mother, knowing I could have avoided this if I had just left him at home? My only

Doctor Karmal's Machine

hope was that the process could be reversed.

Asmond, Glum, Doc, and Doctor Karmal came to join me.

"Is there anything that can be done for Thornbolt?" I asked fighting a tear trying to force itself from my eye.

"Luckily, I have a scroll of flesh to stone." Asmond pulled an ancient looking parchment from the confines of his robes. He unrolled it and began reciting the incantation scribed on it. As soon as he finished, the scroll burst into flames in his hands, completely engulfing it, and to my surprise, not harming Asmond or leaving any ashes. It was as if it never existed.

I had seen the stone warrior at Telk'otu Bend turned into stone and the reverse was no less impressive, as Thornbolt's stone figure slowly became flesh again. My son collapsed to the ground. The strain from being turned into stone and then back to flesh again must have been tremendous.

Glum walked over and checked the Princes limp body. "He didn't survive the transformation." He reached for his magic bag and realized it was in my possession, "I need my book, Sire."

I didn't want to take any chances that I might accidently pull out the crown, so I had everyone turn around as I searched the bag's confines for Glum's book of clerical spells. As with the last time I searched the magical bag, I seemed to find everything but what I was looking for. Finally, I came across the book. I shoved everything I had dug out back into its black depths and tied it around my belt.

"Here Glumstron, you better hang on to this until we have finished our quest." I handed him his book of spells.

I often wondered why Glum read his spells out of a book, while Asmond cast his from memory. While Glum brought Thornbolt back to life, I asked Asmond about this.

"A cleric gained his powers from his god. When the god deemed he was worthy he would empower the cleric with more powers. But, there is a drawback to this. The cleric must read his spells from his book or from a scroll. Whereas, a magician's powers are learned by trial and error. A magician's apprentice learns from his master and studies books, eventually gaining enough knowledge to create his own spells, if he gets strong enough. Some spells are so complex even a mage has to resort to a book or scroll to cast them, and some spells require materials to be cast... such as the scroll I just used. Without the parchment it was written on, it could not be cast, thus making it a one-time use."

Thornbolt came to after being brought back to life. "Why were these arts not taught to Thornbolt? He seems to have been taught everything else."

"The Queen decided against teaching the Prince the arts of magic, since it can be dangerous. As a result, throughout time, very few royalty have attempted to learn my profession."

I returned to the basilisk I had imprisoned and cast another barrier around him. The force field had a limited duration and we could not afford another member of the party having the same misfortune as Thornbolt, since Asmond's scroll was now gone.

By the time I returned to the group, Glum was also on his feet. A spell of *raising the dead* as it was called, took a lot out of the being who cast it, nearly knocking them out in some cases.

We continued on our way toward the Lair of the Gods, being careful to not run into any more swamp creatures, but of course the best laid plans can go astray.

Something is in front of us. It is an intelligence I have never encountered before.

The second Doc finished his statement, a ball of light whisked past my head. It came on me so sudden I was startled and ducked out of reflex. "What the…" It was followed by two more. The balls of light moved exceptionally fast and stopped on a dime. They hovered above our party in a triangular formation.

"What do you want?" Asmond said with a tone of bitterness I had never known him to display before.

"We wanted to see the human stupid enough to attempt to take on Thagoreum," all three balls said simultaneously. As they talked their light turned different colors and glowed brighter with each syllable like someone was turning a dimmer switch up and down to the beat of the strange creature's words. They sounded similar to eight-year-old little girls combined with a magical tone emanating from them.

"Go away, we don't have time for your games. If you bother us again, you might get hurt." Asmond threatened with that same tone, while shaking his staff at them.

The balls giggled and flew off as quickly as they had appeared.

"What were those?"

"The brownie, pixie, and leprechaun of the swamps. They are called will-o'-the-wisps. Very mischievous little creatures that like to lead others astray and get them into bad situations," Asmond responded.

Since I had been on Surrea I had seen or heard several creature's names mentioned that also existed in earth legends and myths. I wondered if there might be a connection with this planet's culture and earth's. I was so wrapped up in finding the Mace of Turmoil and saving the universe from its destruction that I dismissed the thought and did not inquire into the possible connection.

I could sense we were getting near the Lair of the Gods and my pace quickened as I felt drawn toward it. A half hour later I saw a stone structure lurking ahead of us. It looked like something the Aztec's would have built.

We marched up to the temple-like structure. I approached a set of steps that led to the top of it and went into a trance.

"Hiklional huntelkian formaltion balt li'!" I yelled, raising my hands toward the sky. I came out of the trance remembering what just transpired, but not knowing why I said what I had. The ground started shaking and an opening appeared in the steps in front of us... the way into the Lair of the Gods.

"Doc, it's up to you and I." I pulled Sword from

Doctor Karmal's Machine

its sheath and using a strip of rawhide, securely fastened it to my fist. Even if I was knocked unconscious, Sword was going to remain in my grasp. "Let's go. The rest of you stay here, until we return."

Whatever you do, don't look at me. Our victory lies in your hands, or should I say paws, old friend. I chuckled. *Kalena said you have powers you don't realize you have yet and you are the only creature in existence that can destroy Thagoreum. But it will take both of us to bring him down, I imagine. Just remember, stay away from the mace and don't even glance at me.*

I understand Tom, I just hope I don't let you down.

I had Doc walk in front of me as I fished the crown out of Glum's black bag, I unwrapped it and placed it on my head. I tied Glum's bag back on my belt and told Doc to lead on.

As soon as I uncovered the crown, Sword went into the hysterics I had been forced to deal with before. Once I put it on my head, Sword fell silent and I felt different, like I had become a god or something. I felt power and a strength, that even made the Items of Omens seem lame.

I instantly knew the powers I had, but the ones I concentrated on were the powers of the mind, since those were the only ones that would affect Thagoreum.

The hall we walked down was illuminated by an unknown substance that lined the ceiling, similar to the fungus I encountered in the cave below Niat'nuom Live, where I met Omens and found the

Armor of Kim'imota. The walls were lined with hieroglyphics and drawings depicting great deeds and wars of past lives. As we walked farther down the great hall, I looked at the drawings and began to realize they were a chronological history of existence. Something on the wall caught my eye, a sword that looked just like the weapon I grasped in my hand, being held by a King. As I walked along, I began to realize this king had to be King Arthur of the round table.

Sword, do you have a name?

I am the Sword of Kar'itma, the Sword of Omens.

Do you have any other names?

Yes, I am known by many names such as; Durandal, Gram, Joyeuse, Sumarbrandr, Egeking, The Singing Sword, Caladbolg, Excalibur, and Caledfwich. There are many others, would you like to hear them?

No, that is alright. Why didn't you mention these names to me before?

You never asked.

So, the Sword of Kar'itma was Excalibur. I felt a newfound respect for it. As we continued on, I felt a presence in front of us.

There is something in front of us. Doc said at the same time.

We moved cautiously toward an unknown destiny. As we walked down the hall, I could see the wall ending just ahead and opening into a room. That is when I noticed a drawing of Sar'garian and Go'lithum. Just below that was a great war and below that was me fighting Go'lithum while

Doctor Karmal's Machine

Sar'garian watched. I went to the next frame where Doc saved me by snatching the control box out of Sar'garian's hand.

I continued on studying the drawings one by one. The winning of the great war, the Great Reconstruction Council, the Great Feast, my declaration as King of Has'ilon, my marrying La'tian, and on until I returned to earth. Then I saw a black object that looked like a telephone booth surrounded by seven Has'ilon troops. It must be the machine, I thought. Next a drawing of Doctor Karmal and on through the things that happened before and after I arrived back on Surrea. I came to the end of the wall where it showed Doc and I entering the temple and even my studying the wall, the last drawing depicted. A tremendous voice out of the darkness entered into my mind.

It does not show the future, only what has already transpired.

CHAPTER TEN

One Revenge Creates Another

As soon as Doc entered the room it lit up like the Las Vegas Strip. I was right behind him peering into an extremely large dome shaped area about the size of the Astrodome in Houston, Texas. In the center of this enormous room was a platform with the mace sitting on it.

Go ahead, take it, I don't want it anymore.

"The time for games is over, show yourself Thagoreum."

Well, we are even. You know my name and I don't know yours. I can see you and you can't see me. Tell me your name and I will show myself.

"I don't need to see you to know where you are, guardian of the Mace of Turmoil. If you wish to know who I am, consult the wall of history inside your prison. Kalena himself has sent me to gain the mace. I know you and how to defeat you."

I just obtained the information from doc that you seem to have some type of protection against my powers Sterling. The mysterious creature appeared on the opposite side of the colossal room.

He was as large as a two-story house and looked like a cross between a gigantic glob of grayish yellow gelatin and the Brainton I had seen on my first trip to Surrea. A being which looked like a large brain with four stout legs and two antennas with eyes at the ends of them. As he moved he shook and quivered, and I could see no apparent mouth or nose.

I hit it with a mind blast only to have it rebound on me, knocking me back, nearly cold cocking me. I stood up dazed by the backlash I received from my own mental attack. I rubbed my eyes to make sure what I was seeing was real. A transparent beam of pure energy emanated from Doc and Thagoreum. The beams struck each other near the midway point between the two combatants. It looked like two pressurized streams of water on the same linear plane striking each other. The one coming from Thagoreum was the same color as him, a grayish yellow. The one coming from Doc was pure white. The point where the two streams hit was slowly being forced toward Doc.

I threw a mental punch at Thagoreum which caused Doc to gain the advantage as he forced his beam toward the behemoth. Thagoreum countered my attack with one of his own. Once again I was knocked back and dazed. The Crown of Kings went flying off my head from the force of his mental blow.

When I regained my wits, I had a tremendous headache. I quickly realized the crown had been displaced from its resting place on my head. I jumped up searching for the all-important item. I eyed it lying near the wall. I ran for the thing, fighting the pain I was experiencing from my pounding head. Grabbing it and replacing it on my head, I spun to see Thagoreum's beam nearly to Doc.

I started throwing one mental attack after another at the guardian.

I can't... hold out... much... longer.

Realizing Doc was losing, I knew I had to do something quick or all was lost. I made a decision, and hoped it would work. I quickly put the crown back in Glum's bag and made the supreme sacrifice.

I dropped the bag on the ground and teleported to right in front of Thagoreum, in between his beam of mental energy and Doc's. As both beams struck me, Doc's from behind and Thagoreum's in front, I stuck Sword into the gargantuan brain as I felt my lifeforce being destroyed. The last thing I remember was watching the energy from both of them being channeled from me, through Sword, and into the guardian. As Thagoreum screamed, my conscious mind went blank.

I heard a magnificent voice, "Tom. Tom Brown, you must follow me." I opened my eyes and found myself floating in a black void and couldn't tell where the voice was coming from. "Follow the light Tom, it will never lead you astray." Suddenly there appeared a light far in the distance. It looked like daylight at the end of a long tunnel.

I did as the wonderful voice commanded. I don't think I could have resisted it even if I tried, but I don't think I would have wanted to anyway. The light had a beauty that could not be described. It was more like I felt it than saw it.

I floated toward the light, feeling a harmonious symmetry inside my soul that increased as I neared it. The closer I came to the light, which seemed to forever be out of reach, the more wisps of light I saw coming and going from the magnificent flawless glow in front of me. One of these wisps of light approached me. To my amazement and joy it looked like an angel, perfect in every aspect with a long flowing robe and long golden hair.

"Don't be afraid, you are home now." That was all she said, then left me as quick as she came.

I could discern more angels as I approached the irresistible glow. They smiled as they whisked by me. I was dumfounded by the magnitude of what I felt as I entered the awe-inspiring aura. The glow was so bright I dared not look straight at it. Then a voice that made me shake from the respect it deserved spoke to me.

I am the god of Abraham, the creator of all things, the infinite and eternal. I am known by many names, the Holy Trinity, the Lord Jehovah, Yahweh, Allah, Krishna and thousands of others. I am infinite power, wisdom and mercy. I am omnipotent, omniscient and omnipresent. I offer goodness, truth and supreme justice. I am the Lord God.

Another, less important voice spoke to me. *You*

have proved yourself to the Lord, you are his son, for this you shall be punished. The Lord gave the lifeforces you call Omens, La'tian, Glumstron, and Glamrock back to you when the minions of Kaleno, one of the fallen angel's children, destroyed their physical bodies. Now it is your turn to return to the ways of mortal flesh and blood. This is your punishment.

I began to speak but the Lord's servant stopped me. *Do not question these words with mortal understanding, even if God was to answer your question, it would be beyond your comprehension unless the Lord made it otherwise, but you do not deserve such. You must just have faith. When it is time, you shall receive the reward you truly deserve.*

Next thing I knew I was standing in front of Thagoreum with Sword rammed into its hulking frame and he was screaming in pure, absolute agony.

I was knocked back several feet from the raw mental energy that coursed through my body, and fell unconscious.

When I came to, Doc and Thagoreum still fought, although Thagoreum had changed color and seemed to be bloated. He was bleeding from countless places and no longer stood on his legs. They had collapsed from under him. The stalks supporting his eyes drooped, until they nearly touched the ground. I could tell he was dying.

I looked at Doc. He didn't look much better. He was laying on his side with his tongue lying on the ground, bleeding from his nose, and painting fast and hard. He also looked like he was dying.

Doctor Karmal's Machine

I felt he needed my help, so I teleported to the black bag I laid near the wall, on the opposite side of the huge room. I quickly searched its confines frantically looking for the Crown of Kings. I found it and once again placed it upon my head. The power and strength I felt before returned.

One of the crown's abilities was great healing powers. I teleported behind Doc and used the full extent of these wondrous powers. Through the crown I could see Doc's life force slowly leaving his body. It looked like the steam that comes off boiling water. I recalled the life force back to his body and healed the damages to his mind, body, and soul, since I could *see* all three had been severely damaged.

Doc sprang back to life refreshed and revitalized. He got on his feet and renewed his mental barrage against the guardian. Something told me to put the crown away in the magic bag. I watched as Doc slew the great beast. In the end Thagoreum exploded like a large light bulb that had been fed to much electricity. Sparks of raw energy cascaded up into the air to rain down upon our heads.

The dome shaped room slowly became transparent and then disappeared completely. We found ourselves standing in the middle of a large field. The platform that held the mace was the only thing left to testify that the Lair of the Gods ever existed.

The mace was a good hundred feet from us. I turned to see Thornbolt, Asmond, Glum, and Doctor Karmal staring at us in amazement. They were around two hundred feet behind us. I can only imagine how majestic we must have looked to them, knowing we had accomplished a task no other being on the planet could.

I held Sword toward the heavens to signify our victory. The spell was broken as Thornbolt came running toward me. He grabbed and hugged me with all his might.

"I was getting worried father. I don't think I shall ever doubt your being victorious ever again. I used to think all the legends and tales I heard of you might be exaggerated. Now I don't think they probably did you justice. You are truly the greatest warrior in the universe, the King of Kings."

"No son, there is one other who is the only one that deserves the title of the King of Kings." Remembering the title Jesus had claimed.

"Asmond, we travel to the Tal'imon Hills immediately! Doc, instruct Doctor Karmal to take possession of the mace."

Since it would take around three weeks by horseback and even longer on foot, and the carpet could only hold two people, I decided Doctor Karmal would take the carpet while Asmond teleported the rest of the party to Jar'lin. Then they would get Omens and Go'lithum, and meet us at the Tal'imon Hills tomorrow evening. I would keep a respectable distance from the carpet and just keep teleporting to keep the doctor and the carpet within sight. That way if anything harassed the Doctor, I would be there to protect him.

I hoped Kaleno didn't realize we possessed the crown yet. If anything could cause us problems, he could. The doctor and I left for the Tal'imon Hills as the others prepared to go to Jar'lin. Hopefully f Omens and Go'lithum had heard me, but I didn't know for sure. Even though I didn't know if we would need them, I didn't want to take any chances. Go'lithum had proved his worth more than one time to me and an Ancient Golden Dragon was nothing to dismiss either.

As before, once the doctor climbed onto the flying carpet and the command word was given, it took off like it had been shot out of a cannon. As it increased its speed, it became more difficult to keep it in sight. It finally got to the point where I would teleport several miles at a time, just to watch it come and go from one horizon to the other in a matter of seconds.

I hoped the doctor would be able to hold on for the entire trip. I realized nothing on the planet would be able to bother him at the speed he was moving. But on the other hand, if he did slip and fall, I doubted I would see him as he plummeted to his death. Not only that, even if I did see him fall, I couldn't get close enough to keep him from falling to the ground because the mace was securely bound to his waist. If I did get close enough, the mace's curse would make me no longer care if he died. The future of everything that is or will ever be, centered around a frail old man's ability to withstand the trip he was now on.

Once it became dark, something I had not counted on happened. I lost sight of the carpet carrying the good doctor altogether. I tried to judge its speed throughout the night as I teleported from one place to the next. Since I lost sight of the carpet hours ago, I had no idea if I was keeping up with it or not.

I used a trick I learned when I was a boy scout to keep myself traveling in a straight line. I used a star in front and behind me as a point to base where I was going. But, I was taught as the planet rotated, the stars would slowly move. So, I had no idea as the hours went by if I was staying parallel to the carpet or not.

I continued through the night trying to judge the distance and direction of the flying carpet. As daylight hours approached I couldn't see Doctor Karmal's magical ride anywhere. I searched the Surrean sky carefully and slowly my search became more frantic as the minutes rolled by. Then I saw a small speck in the sky, far off to the east of me, moving extremely fast through the atmosphere. Either I had discovered a meteorite, or I had found Doctor Karmal.

As I watched the carpet shoot across the sky, I realized how much easier it was to keep track of at this distance. I teleported to a point where I could make sure Doctor Karmal was still on his magic ride. To my relief, the scientist from the future still clung to his transportation.

I had not slept for over forty-eight hours and felt the lack of sleep taking its heavy toll on my weary mind. I fought the urge to lie down, I could not leave Doctor Karmal alone. The morning hours slowly ticked by as the flying carpet continued its monumental trek across the Surrean sky.

I found it more and more difficult to stay awake as we rapidly approached Jar'lins territorial

Doctor Karmal's Machine

boundary. Finally, the carpet began to slow, letting me know we had reached the meeting place that had been decided upon. I teleported ahead to the farm just outside the Tal'imon Hills to see if the rest of my groups had arrived yet.

Thornbolt, Glum, Asmond, Omens, Doc, and Go'lithum stood waiting for our arrival with the owner of the small farm, Glont Silteon.

"We are ready to finish the quest, Sire," Asmond stated when I appeared. I wasn't, but I had no choice since time was swiftly running out. The carpet carrying Doctor Karmal approached the farm. I gave the command for the carpet to land and it promptly complied with the order. Our party was once again complete. I fought the fatigue trying so hard to overcome me, drawing from within to find the energy to continue with the legendary quest that was in the hands of our small party.

Asmond and I led the final leg of our journey. Twenty-feet behind us was Doctor Karmal, with Omens twenty-feet to his right, Glum and Doc twenty-feet to his left, Go'lithum and Thornbolt twenty-feet behind him. We marched into the Tal'imon Hills in this formation making sure to keep a safe distance from the good doctor and the accursed mace he carried. We continued on our trek until we finally found the One-Handed Bandit of Karti'zone, or should I say, he found us.

"That is far enough, Sterling the Timid. I hope for your wife's sake you have brought the Crown of Kings?"

"I have it, where is my wife?"

"You are in no position to make any demands

Sterling, give me the crown and then if you are lucky I will return your whore back to you with her head intact. Besides, I am tired of her, she doesn't fight when I take her anymore."

"If you laid one hand on her…"

"Because of you, that is all I could touch her with! The crown, or I will start giving her back to you, a piece at a time."

Doc, tell everybody to back away and turn around. Make sure to remind them not to look at me, the bandit, or the crown.

Will do.

A second later Asmond disappeared and Omens, Glum, Doc, and Thornbolt backed away to the spot Asmond materialized.

"Go'lithum, follow Thornbolt and do as he says."

Doc, tell Doctor Karmal to come and get the bag, open it and find the crown within its confines. Pull it out and put it on the ground with the mace.

I laid the magic bag on the ground and turned toward the bandit.

"One-Handed Bandit, my slave is the only one that can resist the crown's beauty. He will put it on the ground for you to take. Then you release my wife once you possess the Crown of Kings, agreed?" I shouted, only to be ignored.

Are you ready Sword?

I am champion of good.

I teleported to where my friends had gathered. Doctor Karmal grabbed the black bag and started searching its confines for the historical crown. He found it and pulled it from the magic bag.

Doctor Karmal's Machine

Doc, tell him to quickly put both items on the ground and run toward us as quick as he can.

Doctor Karmal did as Doc said and sprinted quite well for a man his age.

What are you doing, you can't give it up. Quick go get it! Sword started raving as soon as the crown was revealed, and as I expected, it had the same affect on the man that called himself the One-Handed Bandit of Karti'zone.

The machine appeared in front of the two items, close enough for the mace's curse to affect Jarl Bol'itin. The Kewa's plan was working perfectly. Shortly the machine would be worthless as an item of great magical power. But somehow Jarl withstood the curse long enough to make the threats he made against me a reality.

"I promised you two things, Sterling the Meek. One was the safe return of your wife. You will find her back on the throne in Has'ilon. And second, for you to suffer greatly. Turn around and witness the beginning of the torment I am going to deliver unto you."

I felt drawn to see the threat he promised to deliver. I turned to see my friends standing with their backs to me as I had requested. Thornbolt turned toward me showing pain in his eyes.

"Father..." he pleaded as he stuck his hand out toward me begging for help. To my absolute horror, my son burst into flames and then disappeared into thin air.

"No!" I screamed as tears welled up in my eyes. I turned just in time to see Jarl hop back inside the machine with the crown and mace in his hands.

"I will get you Jarl Bol'itin! I don't care where you go or where you hide, I will get you. Do you hear me scum?" I yelled in pure agony.

"None can say the One-Handed Bandit does not keep his promises. Go home Sterling, I am not through with watching you suffer. You have not heard the last of me yet." His statements were followed by a scream of distress. "What have you done to my machine?"

"Even the gods are against you scumbag. They have destroyed the machine's magical powers. It is no longer going to protect you from my wrath!"

"No, no it cannot be!" He yelled, evidently pushing buttons, pulling levers, and turning dials as the machine performed its normal functions. "Maybe the machine cannot protect me, but the crown and mace can." He appeared between me and the machine. "You do not realize the powers of these two items you gave me, together they almost compare to the machine's might," he claimed triumphantly.

He was half correct. I had no idea what the mace was capable of, but had full knowledge of the crown's powers and knew it had two weaknesses. One, it made the being wearing it psychic and thus susceptible to another psychic. Second, it gave the owner a false sense of security. The first fault was the one I was going to rely on. Since Doc was mentally stronger, it made him mentally superior to Jarl. I knew Jarl could now read my mind, so there was no sense in trying to hide my strategy.

Now Doc!

Jarl did exactly what I expected. He dropped the

Doctor Karmal's Machine

mace and grabbed his head screaming in pain. I didn't waste any time in taking advantage of the situation. As Jarl fought back against Doc's assault on his mind, I used telekinesis on the mace to move it away from the preoccupied bandit, toward the machine. Since the mace was no longer close enough to Jarl to affect him with its curse, he teleported out of his predicament he found himself in. Doc had proved too powerful for him to stand against.

We had won. Doctor Karmal's machine stood motionless waiting for his return. The mace was now inside it, keeping the machine from regaining its magical properties, thus allowing the good doctor to return to his own time, with a tale so amazing he would most likely be committed if he told anybody.

Doc, tell the Doctor to return to his time period. Tell him thank you and I said good-bye and good luck.

We all stood and watched as Doctor Karmal stepped into his technological creation. A couple of minutes later there was a sound like a jet plane as it takes off, then the machine faded out of our lives forever.

Even though we had saved the existence of all things, our task was still incomplete. A scumbag still lived and carried something the great evil desired and I was not about to let Kaleno gain it. Besides, I had a personal grudge against the man that called himself the One-Handed Bandit of Karti'zone. He had killed my only son while I stood by and helplessly watched. I was not going to be robbed of the revenge I felt I needed and I deserved!

I looked at my friends with a cold stare. "Is there any way to track the fiend called Jarl Bol'itin?"

"A Crystal Ball of Location should find him, Sire," Asmond said.

"Where can we acquire one?"

"I have one in my magic shop in Has'ilon, I will be back shortly." As quick as he spoke he disappeared, then a couple of minutes later, reappeared holding a crystal ball.

"Omens. Glumstron, is there any way to bring back my son?" I asked. "Not that I know of Sire," Glum sadly replied.

"I have seen what happened to the Prince once before. I regret to say, his soul was destroyed. I have heard that a being can be brought back to life under almost any circumstances, but once the soul itself is destroyed, nothing can bring them back. The soul is unique unto each creature and cannot be duplicated. It is the personality and life force of your existence," Omens said solemnly.

I went into a fit of depression over the fact my son was gone for good. I didn't want to accept he was gone. I clung to there being something Glum and Omens didn't know that would return him to me. How was La'tian going to react? She would never forgive me for taking him on such a dangerous journey. I was afraid to face her. There is no scorn that equals a woman's wrath, especially a woman's anger over the loss of a child.

I was wallowing in self-pity when Asmond held up the perfectly round and flawless crystal ball. It was the size of a large cantaloupe.

"A Crystal Ball of Location." He meticulously stroked it like he was rubbing the dust off of a priceless artifact. He mumbled and peered into the thing with complete concentration. It began to glow with an eerie blue luminescence, lighting his hands and making his face an uncanny pale blue, even with full daylight directly striking him. No one moved or made a sound, as if we were afraid to disturb Asmond's concentration. Finally, he came out of his trance.

"I have found him."

CHAPTER ELEVEN

You Can't Always Win, or Can You?

"Where is he?"

"He is in the Dwalt Region, near Com'lock."

Of course, these names held no meaning for me. All that mattered was Asmond knew where he was and how to get there.

"How far is Com'lock from here?"

"Ten days by foot," Omens responded. Since I wanted immediate revenge, and the longer we took recovering the crown, the more likely Kaleno would discover its whereabouts, I decided to send Go'lithum back to Has'ilon. He slowed us up considerably and I didn't feel his powers were necessary anyway.

I gave Go'lithum the command to return to Has'ilon on the flying carpet and follow the

Doctor Karmal's Machine

Queen's orders or Glamrock's, whomever was present at the time. He said he understood and would obey. He methodically boarded the magic carpet and gave it the command word to take off.

As Go'lithum floated off toward Has'ilon, Asmond, Omens, Glum, Doc, and I teleported to our fated meeting with the One-Handed Bandit of Karti'zone.

I didn't want him getting away again, so as soon as we appeared in front of the startled bandit, I cast several force fields around us. Sword immediately went crazy from the crown's curse, ranting and raving over wanting to possess it. I had become used to ignoring him, the rest of the group appeared with their eyes closed so they would not be affected.

"I demand revenge, Jarl Bol'itin. I told you it was useless to run or hide from my wrath. Your senseless destruction of my son will not go without consequences. I should have killed you long ago. Prepare to meet your maker!"

Now Doc. As soon as I told Doc to react, I attacked the bandit. Once again, Jarl clutched his head in pain as Doc's mental barrage hit him. I swung Sword at him as he tried to recover from the mental strain he was experiencing. Sword passed through the air. The bandit had made himself intangible through the power of the Crown of Kings. To repay me for my useless attack, he hit me with a fist of force, a very powerful magical battering ram. I flew back into my force field, sliding down it. I felt like I had been kicked in the head by a mule.

I hadn't slept for over fifty hours. I was tired,

fatigued and faint, but my anger burned into me, keeping me going. Sterling the Great was not going to give up that easy. I jumped up with a fire constantly growing inside me, giving me more strength to continue with every second. I was going to get my revenge at all costs.

My rage burned so much now, I was nearly blinded by it. While he was in an intangible state there was nothing I could do that would affect him, unless he was intangible due to being in the astral or ethereal plane of existence.

I teleported behind him, utilizing my armor's ability to travel into those two planes. I swung Sword once again, before the bandit could react to my presence. This time Sword connected and Jarl Bol'itin. The One-Handed Bandit of Karti'zone, was no more. His head flew through the air, leaving his body standing there, refusing to admit it no longer possessed its ability to live. Jarl's body finally not being able to fight the inevitable, slumped to the ground, jerking in the spasmatic dance of death I had witnessed several times on this planet.

His head flew past the point I knew my force fields were, to land in the hands of a grotesque creature, I immediately recognized as a demon of hell. Kaleno had found the crown.

Behind the demon holding the Crown of Kings were twelve other demons, each one different than the other. I was completely exhausted, especially now that my rage had been quenched. I didn't know if I had the strength to fight these new additions to the ever increasingly complicated quest I had

Doctor Karmal's Machine

started on.

"We have company," I yelled as loud as I could.

I wondered if a worn out human fighter, a dwarven cleric, an elven sorcerer, an ancient golden dragon, and a psychic dog would be a match for thirteen nasties from hell. We had no choice. That crown could not fall into Kaleno's hands no matter what the cost.

Doc, quick, attack the one with the crown. He can't escape.

I spurred into action. First, I cast several force fields around all of us. We were spread out over a fairly large area causing my force fields to be stretched to their limits. The first two I cast around both groups. The next couple I used to cut off the remainder of their group from the one possessing the crown, as Doc's mental attack hit the creature from hell.

The face of the demon holding the crown turned from a grin of victory to one of agony as Doc's mind made him go to his knees in pain. I immediately attacked the hell spawn beast while it was being distracted by Doc's mental barrage. Sword flew through the air giving the satanic fiend a fatal wound. Its guts spilled out putting an extremely rancid odor into the air that made me gag from the overpowering stench.

The demon dropped the Crown of Kings as it fell into the dirt face first only to dissipate before my eyes. Being *banished back to hell* as Glum had once put it.

I grabbed the crown and turned to run with the trophy so many had sought, when Doc's inaudible voice entered my thoughts.

Watch out behind you Tom!

I turned, bringing my shield up to block whatever it was Doc warned me about, but unfortunately my response was too slow. Not that the shield would have done me any good. I turned just in time to see the Hollicaustian snap his unholy flail at me. The wicked item entangled me as the last one had before. I went to the ground as the overpowering strips wrapped around my legs, completely ensnaring me.

Omens breathed on the unholy group. Unfortunately, only two of the remaining twelve seemed to be affected by his deadly breath. The Cycloptic Frost Demon and another one just as gruesome, screamed in agony as Omens breath enveloped them. They looked like a match lit by a blow torch as they burned becoming pure flame, then dissipating into nothing as the flames died out.

The rest were totally unaffected by Omens fatal breath of death, even basking in its heat like they felt at home. Asmond disintegrated another demon that stood next to the Hollicaustian holding me in its grip of subjugation.

Three more screamed in pain as they grabbed their heads acting like they were going to explode from Doc's mental attack.

This left six of the hellish party to contend with. The Hollicaustian reached for the crown that I clung to so dearly. I leveled Sword toward it and used the defense that worked so well in the past. I commanded Sword to do its thing and the Hollicaustian found out the hard way I was not as defenseless as I looked. Sword pierced its chest and another evil being was sent back to hell.

I untangled myself from the ownerless flail and I was once again a formidable foe. We were now down to five of them to contend with. Asmond destroyed another demon's spiritual body. At the same time, Doc was hit by some type of spell that put him out of the picture, thus releasing the three he had disabled, allowing them to return to the fray.

There were now seven dangerous nasties facing Asmond, Omens, Glum, and I. Then Omens was hit by a flesh to stone spell causing the Ancient Golden Dragon to be immortalized in stone.

Asmond took his third demon out of the prime material plane of existence. I teleported into the midst of them and sliced two down before I was cold cocked. I slumped to the ground oblivious to the remainder of our monumental struggle.

I came to covered with pelts. There was a roaring fire near enough to be an object of warmth, but not so near as to be a danger. It was dark and I sat up to look into Glum's worried eyes. He had been crying and it made me sad to see such a good and loyal friend in such distress.

"There was nothing I could do. I tried, believe me, I tried. But there was nothing I could do." I had never seen him display this deep of a depression.

I jumped up viewing the area around me. Omens stood motionless, still solid granite, displaying the price he paid for trying to stop the great evil from gaining the Crown of Kings. Doc lay by me, unconscious, but alive, and Asmond was nowhere to be seen.

"Glumstron, what happened?" He ignored me still groveling in self-pity. "Glumstron!"

"Yes, Sire?"

"What happened?"

"After you were hit over the head and knocked unconscious, the battle went against Asmond and I. The four remaining demons were more than Asmond could handle. One of them paralyzed me, so all I could do was watch them overpower him. He fought gallantly against them, you would have been proud. He destroyed two of them before he was finally disintegrated himself. All I could do was watch, there was nothing I could do, nothing, I tried." He started crying.

"What happened to the crown?" I felt like I was in a bad dream.

"The two remaining demons took it and they tried to take your sword, but it shocked them when they tried to pick it up. So, they broke it." To my disbelief he held out Swords two pieces where it had been snapped in half. I stared in shock at the Sword of Kar'itma.

I fell back down totally stunned by the events that had transpired. Thornbolt and Asmond were gone forever, Omens was a stone statue that I had no way of returning to flesh, Doc was down for no telling how long, Glum was currently a manic depressive, Go'lithum was miles away, and I had lost the Sword of Omens, which also meant most of my powers were gone.

CHAPTER TWELVE

The Return of Another Voice in my Head

If I had only stayed out of the middle of them, the outcome may have been different, I would never know. Then suddenly a thought occurred to me, Sword said he could only be destroyed by acid, that meant...

"That meant he was not destroyed and therefore could be repaired." A voice I had heard before, finished my thought for me.

At first, I didn't recognize the voice. I jumped up, spun around, and saw Rewop staring into my eyes. I welcomed the sight of the strange creature that was the last Kewa left alive.

"I am disappointed in you human. You let Kaleno gain possession of the Crown of Kings. If it were not for your success in returning the machine to the future, I would not even be here. For accomplishing that great deed, you have once again proved your worth to the gods, and therefore deserve to be rewarded for your accomplishment. To compensate you, they have sent me to help you regain yourself."

I wondered what he meant by *regain yourself.* Regardless, at this point I was ready to accept any help I could get.

"First off, your hunch was correct. The Sword of Omens has not been destroyed, it can be repaired. You must travel to Kar'itma. There and only there can the sword be made whole again. It must be reforged in the fires it was originally made in. Second, there is one way to bring back your son and Asmond. In the Tullibon Hills is a temple that has long been forgotten. It was built by the first Kewa's to walk Surrea. This temple is called Kew and has an altar deep within its depths which contains the souls of those that have been destroyed. It will be very difficult to reach and very dangerous. In order to regain your son and Asmond, you must first repair the Sword of Omens, then go to Til Norn. Tell him you need a clone of Asmond and Thornbolt. After the two clones are made, take the soulless bodies to the Altar of Dead Souls. Then your two loved ones shall be returned to you. One last thing, do not let anybody other than Til Norn see you while you are in Has'ilon, even your wife."

"I don't understand, why should I not be seen?"

"If you wish to have Thornbolt and Asmond back, do as I say or you will lose them forever."

Doctor Karmal's Machine

Just as soon as he finished the sentence he disappeared.

Once he left, it was as though a spell had been broken, Glum stirred as I turned back toward the camp. Doc was on his feet and even Omens was flesh and blood again.

"How did they…?" Glum started to say with a confused look of amazement etched across his face.

"Didn't you see him?"

"See who?"

"The Kewa."

"Who?"

"Never mind, it is unimportant. We four have another task to do. We go to Kar'itma!"

Since Sword was broken and Asmond was gone, we had to travel the hard way, by dragon back. I explained to Omens what had transpired, while Glum listened. Even though Kar'itma was farther than Jar'lin from our present position, Omens said it would only take three days' time to reach it.

"We leave at first light." I was still totally exhausted, so I lay down and immediately fell asleep.

I awoke to Glum's voice. "Sire, Sire it is time to go."

I opened my eyes as the second Surrean sun rose above the horizon. I jumped up feeling renewed and refreshed. Everybody else was already awake and eating the meal Glum had conjured up. I joined them and quickly devoured the scrumptious feast. Of course the fact that I was famished helped. Shortly afterward we were airborne and headed toward Kar'itma.

Since Omens only had to carry Glum, Doc, and I, and not the weight of Go'lithum, he could fly faster and farther before he had to rest. The countryside rolled by as we swiftly flew toward our objective. We stopped just a few times for Omens to rest and eat, otherwise we were in the air most of the time. Once it became dark we found a good spot and bedded down for the night. Each day was the same as the last and toward the evening on the third day Kar'itma was finally within sight.

We approached the great city as the waning light from the second sun slowly disappeared. The gate guards, unaccustomed to being approached by a dragon, inquired about our business with a tone of caution. Once they noticed me, we were quickly accepted into the city.

Omens polymorphed into a horse to make it easier to traverse the city streets. Within an hour after we had been hailed by the gate guards, we were before Kar'itma's King and Queen.

"Greetings, Sterling. What may I praise for this unannounced call?"

"Har'ital, I am on a quest of great urgency. I am here to ask a favor of my good neighbor." I held out Sword's two pieces. "During a struggle with Kaleno's minions, the Great Sword of Kar'itma was broken. I have been told the only way to repair the Sword of Omens is in the same fire it was forged from. I beg you to grant me this request, my son and Asmond Hir'thito's lives depend on it."

"I shall get my Royal Blacksmith on it immediately. In the meantime enjoy the hospitality of Kar'itma." He called a page, gave him the two halves of the famous sword, and commanded him to deliver them to the Royal Blacksmith with orders to repair the Great Sword of Omens as quickly as possible.

It took several hours for the sword to be mended. While waiting we ate a large feast, watched several dancers, a juggler, some acrobats, and were finally entertained by a court jester who told some pretty bad jokes. I tried to act like they were funny, but since I was and had always been a bad actor, I felt I did as lousy a job as he did. Luckily nobody seemed to notice. Since his type of humor was considered good on this planet, they were all laughing too hard to realize I was faking.

In the middle of one of his worst jokes, I was saved by the proverbial bell, as the page returned brandishing Sword. It shined with the look of being brand new, even more so than the first time I saw it in bright light. I felt like it was an old friend I never expected to see, showing up out of the blue. Once I held Sword and heard his familiar voice speak to me, I became whole again. I was ready to continue with my newest adventure.

Cutting the jester off in mid-sentence, I apologized for my need to go. I thanked the King and Queen for their help and kindness and bid them farewell.

My party was slowly being rebuilt. We stood together and teleported to Has'ilon, under the protection of the midnight sky.

CHAPTER THIRTEEN

The Temple of Kew

Heeding Rewop's warning, I teleported us to a place I knew no one would be, the treasury. I had my three companions wait there for me, as I turned invisible and teleported to the Wizards Guild.

I gave the special knock that only Asmond, Til, and I knew. It told the proprietor inside that the King was outside and was in trouble, needing help.

The tower was magically guarded from outsiders entering it without permission, so I could not teleport into its depths. I just had to wait for the door to be opened from the inside. This structure was Has'ilon's last defense against invasion.

Within seconds from giving the special knock, Til was at the door with a staff in his hands, pointed menacingly at the possible trouble I may have had with me. He had the look of an old man suddenly woken out of a dead sleep, mixed with surprise at hearing a knock he probably never expected to hear.

"Your Highness." He looked straight at me, evidently able to see invisible objects. "Why are you invisible and using the secret knock?"

"Shh!" I hissed as I pushed by him. I saw several guards coming down the deserted street. "Quick, close the door," I whispered and the magician did as I commanded without hesitation.

"Why the secrecy, what is wrong?"

"It is a long story and I do not have time. I need you to do something and I need it quick."

"Your wish is my command. If I can't do it I will find someone who…"

"Yes, yes," I said cutting him off before he could finish his sentence. "I need a clone of Asmond and Thornbolt."

"It will take some time."

"How long?"

"First, I must locate the cell specimens that Asmond has in his magic shop, then it will take around an hour to cast the spell. It is very long and drawn out. Next, the clone will take around eight hours to develop. I figure the clones will be fully grown around noon tomorrow if everything goes right."

"Make it so, I will be back at noon."

"You do realize that unless Asmond and Thornbolt are dead, making a clone of them will drive both the real entity and the clone mad?"

"It is of no consequence, time is running out old

friend, I must go."

"They will be ready by noon, Sire. You have my word."

I teleported back to the treasury. I was worried someone might stumble across my hidden comrades. Since Rewop had warned against letting anybody see us other than Til, I didn't want to take any chances. I teleported us to Telk'otu Bend where we only had the stone statue for company and we spent the night without mishap. As usual Glum was the first one up and had breakfast waiting for us.

We spent the morning hours discussing the events of the past few days. I explained what the Kewa said and inquired into the specifics of cloning. Asmond had the good sense to keep a specimen of each of us before we started our quest. Omens told me, Asmond had informed Til of the whereabouts of our individual strands of hair he procured. They were individually marked, so Til could make a clone of any of us, if needed.

I asked Omens and Glum about the temple of Kew and the Altar of Dead Souls hidden in its depths, but neither one was familiar with it. The morning hours slid by as we discussed first one, then another of the possible places in the Tullibon Hills the Kew may be. Also, the fact that Kaleno now held eleven of the twelve Gems of Godlihood, kept coming up during our discussions, a point that could not be overlooked. If only Go'lithum had been there, the outcome would have surely been different.

Finally, noon arrived and it was time to return to the Silver Hand. Then it occurred to me, how was I going to get inside the magician's guild without being noticed, the city streets would be alive with a flurry of activity. Even invisible, I would surely be seen by somebody capable of detecting invisible objects. Then Glum came up with a solution. He pulled a long hooded black robe out of his bag.

"In case I ever wanted to disguise myself," he said with a smug grin.

I donned the monks robe, tied it securely around my waist with the traditional rope belt attached to it and pulled the hood over my head to completely obscure my features. I was ready to walk Has'ilon's streets incognito.

I materialized outside the Silver Hand, and used the secret knock once again. I had left Omens, Glum, and especially Doc back at Telk'otu Bend, since it would be easier for one to get in and out without being noticed. I tried to look as inconspicuous as possible. The streets were filled with Has'ilon citizens and travelers passing through. One roving merchant did his best to get me to buy his "golden fruit" as he called it. I said no and ignored him as the heavy reinforced door swung open propelled by Til's hand.

Til had that unmistakable look of one who had not gotten enough sleep. He motioned for me to enter, as I dodged the peddler to get inside the safety of the Silver Hand's boundaries. The door closed and I finally felt at ease, protected from detection by the nearly impregnable walls of the Silver Hand.

Til led the way down into the depths of the keep. Not only did the tower rise above ground, but there were also several levels below ground. We walked into the large room containing the fully developed clones of Asmond and Thornbolt.

"I have some bad news Sire. For some unknown reason I have never experienced before, these clones did not respond to me. It is as if they are zombies, oblivious to their surroundings. Like their souls were destroyed or something."

"Their souls were destroyed."

"Then why the clones? Once a soul is destroyed, it cannot be regained." Til's face had the look of total horror, obviously shocked from the apparent loss of his mentor and the Prince.

"There is a way to regain a destroyed soul, but I do not have time to explain, I must be off." I said good-bye to the old man and returned with the two lifeless bodies to my friends who were anxiously waiting for me.

Since we had no idea where to start looking in the Tullibon Hills for the Temple of Kew, I teleported our group to the center of the vast expanse known by this name.

We used Glum's Stone of Direction to gain a bearing on which way to begin our search for the ancient temple. It pointed to the southeast from our present position. We wasted no time in following its guidance and we quickly covered a large distance as I teleported our party from one place to another.

After several hours of hopping from one point to another we zeroed in on a lone hill the stone pointed to from all sides. The hill was either the Temple of Kew or camouflaged it, one of the two.

We searched the entire hill looking for some type

Doctor Karmal's Machine

of entrance. Finally the Stone of Direction led us to a large boulder located at the foot of it.

After Glum carefully examined the boulder, he came to the conclusion it was some type of door. We searched for some way to open it. After a good hour of scrutinizing the thing, we gave up and I decided to disintegrate it. The disintegrate spell disrupted the boulder's molecules showing us the hallway it had kept hidden so well. We entered the ancient temple and proceeded in the direction the stone pointed.

It was a magnificent relic of past ages. Everywhere I looked, the walls, ceiling, and floor were covered with drawings, hieroglyphics, and scriptures of all sorts of design and color. I felt like an archaeologist that had discovered the ancient tomb of some great Egyptian king.

We traversed hallway after hallway, traveling ever deeper into Kew's confines. About an hour after we entered the ancient temple, the stones shook violently throwing us to the ground. Other than a spell that a cleric cast when I fought Sar'garian and his minions in the Great War, this was the first time I had experienced an earthquake on Surrea.

It only lasted a couple of seconds, but was severe enough to crack the walls, ceilings, and floors of this unique temple built ages ago. At first it didn't hit me, but then I realized I had not seen a crack anywhere inside this structure before, but now it was covered with them. It was as though the Gods protecting this temple had been angered by us defiling its age-old seclusion.

We continued on our search for the Altar of Destroyed Souls, going ever deeper into Kew's depths. The stone of direction guided us flawlessly. The temple was immense, much larger than it looked from outside. Glum said we had been gradually going down an incline, and were deep below the surface now.

About an hour and a half after we entered the temple another tremor hit, just as violent as the last one and lasting twice as long. This time the place started to crumble around us. Considering how intense the tremors were, it was a wonder the temple had not fallen down on top of our heads. I wondered, considering the damage already taken, if it would be able to withstand another tremor before it finally succumbed to the violent pounding it was being forced to endure.

I had a feeling the tremors were not over, so we quickened our pace sensing an urgency to complete our journey as quick as possible. The complex seemed to not have an ending to its intricate maze.

I heard something up ahead, but I don't sense anything, nor am I locating any intelligence nearby.

"Maybe it was just a piece of ceiling falling or something," Glum said in response to Doc's warning.

Glum's suggestion was logical, but I still proceeded with extra caution, just in case. I had learned to rely on Doc's warnings. So far, he had not given a false one, but there was always a first time for everything.

The hall we were in opened into a large room. The stone pointed to a hallway on the opposite side and we hurried toward our objective. As soon as we were halfway across the two-hundred-foot diameter room, we were attacked by thirty or more nasties coming at us from all sides. They seemed to come out of the woodwork. They looked like human corpses someone dug up after they had decayed for a while and been given back their lives without regenerating their rotten tissue.

"Zombies!" Glum shouted, which is exactly what I would have called the unnatural creatures. One of the rare times I actually made a lucky guess. He started thumbing through his book.

Omens breathed his deadly fire to our right, engulfing about ten of them in a blaze of red hot flames as they closed in. The Zombies moved and attacked quite slowly making it very easy to defend against their outstretched hands. I stabbed the first one to approach me in the chest. Sword seemed to have no effect on the gruesome creature. It didn't even bleed and Sword didn't have a drop of blood present when I withdrew it from the undead thing.

"They're already dead, you can't kill them again! Fire is the only thing that will destroy them besides magic," Glum shouted as I severed one of its arms. To my surprise the arm hit the ground and had a life of its own as its fingers dragged the appendage toward me, while the zombie didn't even seem to notice it had lost it. To make matters worse, several more Zombies came out of the darkness.

"They're fire resistant!" Omens exclaimed in horror.

There were now around fifty slowly converging on us. Omens was useless against them and I only had a few spells that would affect them. I was just about to put up a force field in a circle around us for protection when Glum spoke.

"This is my area of expertise Sire, let me handle them."

"No problem, be my guest." I backed up to allow Glum to do his thing, whatever that might be.

He began a chant out of his book and started to glow with a bright, pure white light. It looked like somebody had placed a powerful fan underneath him as his robe, hair, and beard blew straight up. His voice became very loud as the chant continued.

The zombies started screaming and looked to be in severe pain. He raised a hand toward the ones in front of him and a beam of the strange white light emanated from his fingers splitting into multiple bolts to hit several of the undead creatures in the chest. These bolts of light passed right through them to strike others behind them. Once the light hit the chest, it quickly engulfed their entire body. The zombies became creatures of pure light and as the light dimmed, the unholy things disappeared into nothingness.

The rest of the zombies fled before they befell the same fate as their comrades. I knew Glum better than anyone else I had met on Surrea, and he still managed to surprise me.

Just as soon as the remaining zombies fled another quake hit. It had been about fifteen minutes since the last one and this was twice as long. The time between them was cutting in half and the duration was doubling.

The newest tremor leveled a wall in the room

Doctor Karmal's Machine

where we stood. Several blocks fell from the ceiling and a huge crack opened up in the floor. The Temple of Kew was slowly being destroyed by an unknown force. As soon as the tremor quit we started running toward our objective, only stopping long enough to consult the stone when we found it necessary. None of us said it, but we all knew the temple was falling in around us.

About eight minutes later another tremor hit, twice as long as the last one and more violent. The ceiling caved in behind us and I had to put up a force field to protect us from falling rubble. As we continued on our way, the going became more difficult now that large pieces of stonework blocked our path here and there. I found it necessary to teleport the group past areas impossible to get by on foot.

We came out into a large room, twice the size as the last one. It was in the shape of the inside of a pyramid. The ceiling got lost in the darkness above us and was also obscured by a heavy mist above our heads. A beam of energy came down through the center of the room to fall on a stone shrine. This beam contained the colors of a rainbow swirling around, mixing together to create other colors, only to separate again. It was one of the prettiest sights I had seen yet on this wonderous planet.

The Stone of Direction pointed straight at the shrine that was lit by the beautiful light in the center of the huge room. We had found the Altar of Destroyed Souls.

We started for the altar when another quake hit just four minutes after the last one. It was by far the most violent yet and I noticed the beam acted like a light with an electrical short in it, as it flickered on and off in rhythmic spurts that seemed to coincide with the quakes tremors. The Altar of Destroyed Souls was losing its powers.

"Quick, get Thornbolt on the altar!" I commanded Omens, who had been carrying our two lifeless companions. I figured we had about 2 minutes before the next tremor hit. Not knowing how long it took for the soul to be replaced, or if it would harm them if they were inside the beam if it flickered on and off, I just hoped we still had time.

Omens started for the altar when a tremendous voice came bellowing out of the darkness.

"Who dares to defile my temple?"

"Show yourself," I said without thinking. I stood ready to defend us against this newest threat if it became necessary.

"I am the guardian of Kew. I answer to no one, especially an insignificant human. If you wish to remain nameless, so be it. Regardless, you have caused the destruction of this ancient temple and shall be punished for your sacrilege. Prepare to meet Qualitian the Unconquerable."

"Omens, get them on the altar. I will deal with our friend. Inequality the Conquerable, I don't know who you have dealt with in the past, but now you face Sterling the Great, the strongest warrior in the universe, champion of good!"

Omens started to move toward the Altar of Destroyed Souls as I moved in the direction of the voice that belonged to the unseen creature. Before Omens could reach it he, Thornbolt, and Asmond went flying through the air like they had been hit by some unseen force.

Its invisible. Sword said as he made the being become visible to me.

I was unprepared for what I was seeing. He looked like a giant but was far more immense than any I had viewed before. He was at least forty-foot tall, wore chainmail, held a fifteen-foot sword, and a twelve-foot shield that looked small in comparison to his massive frame. There was enough material in one of his leather boots to make a three-piece outfit for me, with enough left over to make a pair or two of size ten boots.

It is a Titan. Don't let his sword hit you, it will sheer right through the Armor of Kim'imota.

Gee, thanks. As if I needed that bit of information. *No, I was planning on checking the armor's ability to withstand it.* I don't know why I was being so sarcastic to Sword. I guess I was not sure if I was going to be able to handle this monstrosity and was just taking my worries out on him. *Can the Shield of Jar'lin repel its blow?* I asked in a more serious tone, evidently regaining some of my confidence.

It should. Not exactly the answer I was looking for. The *should* part bothered me. Regardless, I had a feeling I was going to find out whether I liked it or not.

The Titan took one step to cover the twenty-five-feet between, us cutting the distance down to seven.

Go to your full length. I commanded Sword as I took a swipe toward the titan's ankle. At the same time the titan swung his massive sword in an arc toward my body.

Sword lengthened to twelve-foot. Its razor-sharp edge cut into the titan's leather boot and buried itself into its ankle. At the same time the giant sword came flying toward me and I just managed to block it. Even its enormous size, coupled with the massive strength of the creature, was rebounded by the unique properties of the Shield of Omens, without me feeling any part of the blow.

The titan's sword flew back the way it had come having the same effect on him that it would on a regular sized human. The titan was thrown off balance and screamed from the gash Sword had made in its huge ankle. There was a six-inch-deep cut, which equated to a three-quarter inch deep slash in a normal sized leg. Not devastating, but bad enough to impair.

Between the cut in his ankle, being thrown off balance from his sword rebounding back at him, and the quake that decided to hit at the same instant, the colossal creature went down. He hit so hard and fast, he left an imprint in the stone floor, adding to the ferociousness of the tremor.

The quake was so violent all of us went to the ground, as it brought the temple raining down on our heads. It was about two minutes since the last tremor and I knew our time was quickly running out. To make matters worse, the beam of energy stopped completely during the quake.

I cast a force field to protect us from the large stone blocks falling from above, just as one fell on the titan's head, crushing it. We would never know which one of us was more powerful than the other.

Doctor Karmal's Machine

The quake stopped and so did our hearts as the four of us stared at the Altar, no longer radiated by the unusual beam of light emanating from the hidden roof above. Then, like a fluorescent light flickering as it comes into being, the spectacular beam once again gave an eerie form of life to the Altar of Destroyed Souls.

We rushed Thornbolt and Asmond's soulless bodies to the altar. I picked up Thornbolt and laid him on the stone shrine, praying there was enough time to return his soul to his body.

His limp body lay silently on the stone slab. At first nothing seemed to happen, but then his inanimate frame absorbed the beam, making it glow until it radiated a similar light.

Thornbolt's body began to vibrate lightly at first, slowly building into a violent shake as his body flopped around on the Altar of Destroyed Souls.

Finally, he opened his mouth to produce a faint whisper that quickly became a loud scream of absolute agony. Then tears came to his eyes as he looked into mine and he faintly said, "Father". My son had been returned to me.

Thornbolt was too weak to walk, so I helped him down from the altar. As Glum began to place Asmond upon it, we were once again thrown to the ground from another quake.

I cast another force field above our heads to stop the ever-increasing amount of rubble cascading down around us. I didn't want one or more of us to meet the same fate as the titan. The altar room's floor was covered with the enormous blocks that had fallen from above, and once again the rainbow-colored beam stopped blazing.

The tremor ended and I held my breath waiting for the beam of light to flicker with life again. Nothing happened.But, just when I was about to give up hope, the beam crackled into existence, possibly for the last time.

We put Asmond's body upon the stone slab and watched as the miraculous beam slowly gave him back his lost soul, as it had Thornbolt.

When he began screaming the next quake hit, cutting off the beam of light again. Asmond continued to scream in agony as the quake shook the temple. This time it began to literally fall to pieces. I waited as long as I felt was possible, then came to the realization the quake was not going to stop and the temple was going to crumble into dust.

I teleported the party outside, while Asmond continued to scream hysterically. The process of his soul being returned to his body was not complete, and would never be. The hill hiding the Temple of Kew collapsed, forever burying the Altar of Destroyed Souls.

I didn't know whether to cry for joy because I had regained my only son, or weep in sorrow because I had lost a good friend. I silently did both.

"Is there anything anybody has heard of that can be done for Asmond?" Receiving no answer from my disenchanted friends, we stared in disbelief at Asmond as he screamed in excruciating torment.

"Sage of Zer'ical," Asmond yelled to everybody's surprise.

"Of course, why didn't I think to ask the legendary Sage of Zer'ical. Maybe he can help end

Asmond's suffering," Omens exclaimed.

"Where can we find this sage?" I asked renewed with a ray of hope.

"He lives somewhere in the Hor'kuth Mountains."

"To the Hor'kuth Mountains it is."

I remembered the mountain range quite well. It was where I met La'tian, Omens, and had found the Armor of Kim'imota. We gathered together and I teleported us to the base of the great mountain range, near its center.

CHAPTER FOURTEEN

The Witch of the Cloud of Moons

Traversing the dangerous range would be a thousand times simpler than the last time I scaled its perilous cliffs. I had the ability to teleport now and didn't have that versatile and handy power then.

Over the course of several hours, we narrowed the legendary sage's position down to a lone mountain, using the Stone of Directions guidance. An hour later we were standing in front of a large cave opening, while Asmond's incessant screaming announced our arrival.

"Sage of Zer'ical!" I yelled as loud as I could to be barely heard over Asmond's screaming voice. "We are in need of your ultimate wisdom and knowledge," I screamed, barely out doing Asmond's shrill shriek of torment.

Doctor Karmal's Machine

Suddenly, Asmond fell silent. I looked to see him still going through the motions of his constant scream, yet nothing seemed to be leaving his gapping mouth.

"What do you require Sterling of Surrea, Tom Brown of Earth?" A voice came out of the dark recesses of the cave, that resembled Til Norn's elder cackle. "Maybe a little help restoring Asmond Hir'thito to his former self, eh? It will cost you dearly for my knowledge, Sterling the so called Great."

"What do you want? I will give you anything."

"Anything did I hear you say? Yes, I do believe you said anything."

"As long as it is within my power to give to you, yes, anything."

I owed Asmond everything. Not only was he a dear and loyal friend, but he'd given me what no other had, a chance to prove myself to myself.

"I want the Crystal Orb of Knowledge. Bring it to me and I will complete the return of Asmond's soul."

"Where is this orb you speak of?" I was beginning to wonder if I would regret my rash statement.

"The witch called Baldnon has it. Her castle is in the Cloud of Moons. But I warn you, she will know you are coming. She has great knowledge through the orb's powers. Leave Asmond here, I will protect him until your return."

"Where is the Cloud of Moons?"

"Up in the sky. Don't you know anything?" he asked quite sarcastically.

"I know where the evil place is, Sire. You may want to leave Glumstron and Thornbolt behind also, it is a very dangerous place."

I agreed with Omens wisdom. I had lost Thornbolt once and did not want to lose him again.

"Sage of…"

"Yes, yes, you can leave them behind also. They will be safe with me."

Omens, Doc, and I teleported to the Cliff of Despair, at the very northern tip of the known world, just above the Swamp of Turnos. Omens said the Cloud of Moons could be seen from the thousand-mile-long bluff.

As we stood on the great cliff, it looked like the edge of a flat world. The basin far below was completely obscured by a heavy mist that resembled clouds, which added to the effect. The cliff was virtually a perfect ninety-degree angle straight up from the ground, which had to be over one mile below our feet.

Any direction away from the Cliff of Despair looked like the top of a slowly moving cloudy scene. Far off in the distance was a black castle that seemed to be floating on top of the clouds.

Omens pointed toward the gloomy castle. "The Cloud of Moons."

Since the castle was protected from someone teleporting to it, Doc rode on Omens back in the special harness we had made for him, while I flew under the powers of the Items of Omens. As we approached the evil fortress, the more wicked it looked, like a haunted castle out of the dark ages.

When we came within a hundred feet, the

Doctor Karmal's Machine

drawbridge lowered, welcoming us, giving me an uncanny, ominous feeling. We landed on the eerie drawbridge and Omens polymorphed into a smaller version of himself. We walked into the castle's ghostly depths as if we owned the place.

I had been on enough ventures for one month and didn't feel like playing hide and seek with the witch I was looking for. So, I yelled as loud as I could. "Baldnon, you know we are here. Show yourself so I can complete the quest I have started!"

"You are overconfident, Sterling. I know why you are here, warrior. But that foolish sage has only sent you to your death, like the many others he has tricked before you. For a hundred years he has attempted to gain what is rightfully mine, and for a hundred years has failed miserably. I know each of your strengths and weaknesses. You cannot win, but you will still try, won't you?" Her voice came out of the castle's depths and was a creepy crackled one that made my flesh crawl and my hair stand on end.

"Now you sound overconfident. Baldnon, show yourself and let the games begin!" She was not going to shake my confidence in my abilities.

"Funny you should use the word *games*."

As she finished the sentence I heard a loud click above me. Without thinking and before I even looked up to see what made the sound, I cast a force field above our heads to protect us. As my gaze was drawn upwards, a cascading waterfall of red liquid hit my dome shaped barrier and began to flow down it. I cast several more force fields to back up the first one, just as it disappeared.

"Curse your lousy ring!"

When she said that, my gaze landed on the Ring of Kal'ijora and I noticed it was glowing. The red liquid slid down the barrier to finally hit the ground eating into the stone. The Ring of Omens had taken over my thoughts to protect Sword from complete destruction, not to mention what the acid would have done to us.

"What's the matter Baldnon? Doesn't your orb tell you what the Ring of Kal'ijora is going to do?"

"That ring is not going to save your life dragon dung."

Luckily, once we were past the entrance my teleport spell worked like normal, so I moved us into the hidden depths of the dark castle, as far as I could see in front of me. The section of the floor we had been standing on disappeared as a large block of stone fell from above it.

"Curses!" She cackled when her plan had been foiled again. Only this time it was by me, not the ring.

She is above us on the second level of this complex. Docsaid.

I teleported us to the stairway I could barely see, looming ahead of us in the shadows. Since teleportation was extremely dangerous without seeing or having seen exactly where you wanted to go, I couldn't teleport straight to her without risking materializing inside something solid, thus killing one or more of us. Because, none of us had been inside this place before, I was forced to teleport within eyesight.

We hopped from one spot to another, as Doc led us to her whereabouts through his unique mental powers. We quickly made it to the second story of the eerie fortress and Doc led us toward her location.

She is on the other side of that door.

At the end of a hall was the door Doc referred to. I teleported us to it and threw it open., We recklessly charged into the dimly lit room ready for action.

It's a trap, get... But before he could finish the warning, Sword suddenly became very heavy, the same weight I felt the day I first held him in my hands. A large metal portcullis fell behind us barring the door startling us as it slammed into place.

"I told you, you couldn't win Sterling. Even your psychic beast and the ring can be tricked. Good-bye so called Champion of Good, you have met your match in Baldnon, Sorceress of the Dark Powers." The witch chattered on as a sound of machinery made its way to my ears.

"The ceiling!" Omens said with a tone of horror.

I looked up to see a thousand-pointed steel spikes slowly coming out of the ceiling. They were set about an inch apart from each other, leaving nowhere to hide. The walls, floor, and ceiling were all made out of the same metal as the spikes inching their way toward us.

I tried to teleport out of our fatal predicament, but nothing happened. I turned and cast a disintegrate at the metal portcullis, again nothing. I even tried a force field above us, to stop the metal rods from continuing their fatal trip toward us, but to no avail.

"We have big problems guys, none of the Items of Omens seem to be functioning."

"Neither are mine, I tried to polymorph, but nothing happened. It must be some kind of anti-magic shield."

I ran to the metal grate separating us from death and safety. I tried to lift it but couldn't even budge it., I swung Sword with all my might, barely nicking it when Sword hit. If I had the time, I could eventually hack our way out, but time was one thing we didn't have on our side.

"Let me try something, Sire. Hopefully my breath still works."

I stepped back as he moved up to the grating. He took a deep breath then let it out slowly in a concentrated stream. His intense heat quickly turned the metal rods cherry red. I looked up at the steel spikes, they were half way to us. Time was quickly running out. Luckily, they moved at a very slow rate. My guess, on purpose, just to mentally torture whoever was unlucky enough to get trapped inside the room, before they were impaled.

The metal rods started to sag. Omens ran out of wind and took in another deep breath. He continued his relentless assault against the obstinate metal unwilling to release its prisoners.

I had to duck down as the spikes reached my head. The metal rods began to melt and drops of molten metal hit the floor. The spikes were down to five-foot when Omens took in his third deep breath. I was on my hands and knees next to Doc as we watched our only possible salvation work away at the stubborn metal. Finally, when the steel spikes

Doctor Karmal's Machine

were inches away from Omens miniaturized frame, most of the portcullis became so hot, the rods turned to liquid and flowed to the ground.

There was now a large hole in the steel grating. We had a way out. Since we didn't have time to wait for the metal to cool, I stuck the Shield of Omens up as an umbrella to protect us from the molten drops that continued to rain down from the melted grate. Doc leapt across the molten river on the ground and Omens followed him.

Once he was outside the special room, Omens regained his powers and polymorphed himself into a human so he could hold the shield to protect me as I left the room. The magic elven boots I was wearing would not protect me from the molten lead, so I dived out of the room and rolled to safety. We had escaped the witches fatal trap unscathed.

I sense her nearby, she thinks we are dead and is gloating over her victory.

How close? I asked Doc with a thought.

Just down the hall.

I teleported us silently to the spot indicated by Doc and threw the door open on the startled witch. She looked ugly and grotesque, just like what I would have expected a witch to look, down to the large wart on her long-pointed nose. Her hair was long, white, and sparse like she had undergone radiation treatments. The old frail frame was covered with a black tattered robe and she wore the pointed hat traditionally portrayed by earthly legends. What really got me was she stood in front of a large black boiling cauldron and held an old broom in her left hand while thumbing through a large black book with her left. I almost laughed but was shocked at the same time about how much the scene before me matched the Hollywood stereotypes.

"How did you escape my inescapable trap?"

She glanced to her left and with startling speed for such a decrepit looking old woman, reached for a golden ball sitting on a shelf, only to be foiled by an invisible field protecting it from her grasp. As soon as I realized what she was reaching for, I cast a force field around it. I had beaten her to the punch.

"No!" She screeched and turned menacingly toward us. "You shall pay for your insolence."

She grabbed her head as if in pain, while Omens blew his deadly breath at her. The dragon breath had no effect on the witch, and she retaliated against Doc's mental attack with a wave of her hand.

Out of the corner of my eye, I saw Doc transform into a large toad. She waved her hand again and the toad and Omens both froze in their places. It was now just the two of us. I teleported across the room to stand beside her.

I swung Sword at the evil witch only to pass through her intangible body. She waved that deadly hand again and I went flying through the air like I had been hit by a giant's club. I slammed into the wall and slid down slightly dazed. She waved her hand over the barrier keeping her from obtaining the Crystal Orb of Knowledge, which is what I expected the golden ball to be, only to be stopped by another force field I barely had time to cast.

She screamed, her frustration and anger apparent. I cast a disintegrate at her. It reacted on her like I have never seen before. She screamed again, but this time as if in pain. She stumbled back and seemed to age before my eyes. I followed it with another, to be rewarded with the same results.

I slowly walked toward her and cast another disintegrate at the wicked witch. She dropped to her knees and lost her hold on the old broom as it fell to the floor.

The broom, get the broom. It is the source of most of her powers, Sword said as she reached for the old relic.

I hit her with another disintegrate, knocking her back and away from the old broom lying on the ground and used a telekinesis spell on it. The broom flew through the air into my waiting hand.

Break the broom.

Grabbing the ancient thing I started to bring it down onto my knee to snap it in half when the witch begged in agony.

"No! I beg you, don't break it."

"Release my friends and maybe I won't."

"I cannot without my broom."

I was not going to be tricked that easy. "I gave you your chance." I once again started to bring the broom down onto my knee.

"Okay! Okay, I will do as you say, just don't break it, I beg you."

She waved her hand and the toad turned back into Doc, then both Doc and Omens once again stirred.

"Omens, get the crystal orb," I commanded as I held the broom ready to snap it if she tried anything.

Omens went over and grabbed the golden orb.

Then he and Doc came over to stand beside me.

"You have the crystal orb and your companions back, now keep your promise and give me back my precious broom."

In the past I would have given her back the ancient broom, but Jarl Bol'itin had taught me a valuable lesson. Mercy had no place on Surrea, it would only come back and haunt you, as he did.

"I never said I would give it back, I just said I might not break it."

I brought the broom down on my knee, snapping it like a twig. The witch watched horrified and just as soon at the broom snapped she screamed in agony and melted before my eyes, until only her robe and hat were left. Baldnon was no more.

"We have a date with a sage," I said triumphantly as I teleported us back to the sage's abode in the Hor'kuth Mountains.

CHAPTER FIFTEEN

The Return of an Invisible King

We materialized in front of the cave where the Sage of Zer'ical lived.

"I have returned!" I yelled into the dark recesses of the cave.

Thornbolt ran out to welcome us back. "Father!"

"Welcome back, Sire," Glum said as he too came out of the darkness behind Thornbolt.

"The crystal orb, you have the Crystal Orb of Knowledge. Quick, let me have it, I must have it."

"First, return Asmond's soul to him."

I heard a familiar voice come out of the darkness, as Asmond walked out into the sunlight. "It has already been done, old friend."

"As soon as you left I gave him back his sanity. Even if you would not have succeeded in gaining the Crystal Orb of Knowledge, I would have returned him back to his old self. Asmond and I have been good friends for a thousand years." He laughed like he had tricked me. "As a reward for gaining the most prized item any sage could ask for, I will give you two pieces of knowledge you can use, Sterling the Great." He laughed again, only in a happier tone this time.

"Which do you want first, the good news or the bad news?"

"The bad, I guess."

"You will find your kingdom a little different than you left it. Your wife is alive but different, and now that the machine is gone, nothing in the universe can change her back. The good news – there is a way for you to return to your Earth. One item is the only thing in existence known to be able to open the dimensional portal between Surrea and Earth. When you are ready to return, come seek me out and I will help you find it."

I didn't know what he meant by my kingdom and La'tian being different. I started to imagine all sorts of things that may have happened. Jarl Bol'itin had said my suffering was not ended by Thornbolt's demise and Rewop had warned me against being seen in my own kingdom. I put two and two together, realizing Jarl's threat, Rewop and the sage of Zer'ical's warnings all added up to one thing, trouble. The adventure I thought was over several times now, seemed to become more and more complicated all the time. As far as returning to earth, I had already decided to stay on Surrea with my wife and son till the end of my natural life.

Doctor Karmal's Machine

"Explain what you mean by this," I demanded.

"Go to your 'used to be home' and discover for yourself. If I told you the truth, you would do the same anyway. Experiencing is the best way to gain knowledge. Now keep your side of the bargain and give me the crystal orb."

"First tell me what I want to know, then I will give it to you. You have the word of King Sterling."

"No, it was not part of the bargain."

"It is now!"

"Give the orb to Asmond, then I will tell you what you want to know. But I warn you, it will not be to your liking."

Reluctantly, I did as he said, feeling like it might be some type of trick.

He is the real Asmond, Doc reassured me. Besides, if it was a trick, I would make the sage pay for his insolence.

"Your wife, Queen La'tian has been changed through the power of the machine. She will hate you with all her might and want you dead. Otherwise, she is unharmed and unchanged. You no longer have a home on this world, Sterling. Your kingdom is no longer yours, unless of course you banish the Queen from it."

I stood listening to his words in disbelief. If what he said was true, I no longer did have a home on Surrea. Just as he said, I would have to find out for myself.

"We return to Has'ilon!"

We materialized in the throne room. It was around four in the afternoon and the Queen was sitting on the throne, conducting business as usual.

An emissary from the Harluthian Kingdom was standing before her, evidently discussing some sort of treaty. I looked at the most beautiful woman I had ever seen, the one I had taken for my bride.

She was concentrating on her current business and didn't notice us appear, but others did. A hush came over the large assembly and then a low murmur erupted, the King and Prince of Has'ilon were back.

A court advisor leaned over and whispered in her ear. She burst off the throne, rudely ignoring the diplomats before her.

"My son and husband, where?" She asked trying to suppress the tears of joy, that ran down her cheeks anyway.

Maybe the Sage of Zer'ical had been wrong, I thought. She seemed to be overjoyed with happiness at our return. Then I found out the hard way to never doubt the wisdom of a sage.

"Thornbolt my son, Sterling my..." She stopped as her gaze fell upon me. Her whole personality changed from happiness to absolute anger and disgust. "You! How dare you come here. Guards kill him!" She yelled hysterically, while pointing her finger toward me.

The guards spurred into action by their Queen's hostility, searched the room looking for the reason for her outbreak of extreme rage.

"Kill who, Highness?"

"The killer holding my son!"

"But, the only one next to Prince Thornbolt is King Sterling, there is no other."

"Yes, he is the one, kill him, I order you to kill

him!"

"But your Highness?"

"Do as I say or I will have your head!" She screamed madly, as she turned toward my loyal soldier with an insane look in her eyes. Just as soon as she took her gaze off me, the insane rage left her. She looked at the soldier with a perplexed look on her face.

"What is wrong sergeant, you look like you have seen a ghost?" She said calmly.

The entire room watched the Queen in disbelief, wondering what she would do next.

"Did someone say my son and husband had returned?" She said eyeing the room with a look of puzzlement, until her gaze once again settled on me. The rage returned, as she pointed at me and once again ordered my destruction.

I turned invisible and as I expected the rage disappeared. Her gaze fell on Thornbolt.

"Son!" she exclaimed joyfully, stretching her arms out expecting him to come running to her so she could give him a hug. The Prince just stood there, while her look of joy turned into one of concern.

"Go to her, son."

"But father?" He questioned, evidently frightened by his mother's actions.

"It is alright, go."

Thornbolt ran to his mother's outstretched arms and her worried look was again replaced with one of joy.

"I was told King Sterling had returned, where is he?" She stated through the tears that had begun flowing.

"I am here La'tian," I said sadly, knowing that La'tian could never see me again.

"Where my King. I cannot see you." She searched the room longingly.

"Asmond, Glumstron, Omens, explain to her what has happened, I don't have the heart to."

The three of them explained in great detail the events that had transpired since her abduction by the One-Handed Bandit and Doctor Karmal's machine. The entire assembly, including the Harluthian diplomats, were glued to their tales of the great deeds we had accomplished.

When Omens told of the sage's words about the curse placed on the Queen, the faces of everybody present showed an understanding of the Queen's actions, relieved to know she had not gone crazy. He finished at the point of our arrival to the throne room. La'tian could not believe she would want me dead, until I finished the rest of what had transpired since our return.

"So, you see La'tian, I must leave Has'ilon for good. The kingdom cannot be run by an invisible King. I must return to my planet."

"I would still be happy to be with you, even if I couldn't see you. And I don't think it would matter to your subjects whether they could see you or not. Please stay my King, I beg you."

"I cannot, I must return to my home."

"I understand, I will always love you Sterling."

"Asmond, I am ready, send us home."

"Uh, well, you see, I, uh, can't," he said, choking on each word.

Doctor Karmal's Machine

"What do you mean you can't?"

He explained to me how the portal between our dimensions had closed and would not open again for eighty-nine more years. I stood flabbergasted by his words and realized I had one more adventure to complete before I could return home. Now I knew why the sage told me what he had called 'the good news'. I had to return to the Sage of Zer'ical before I could return to earth.

I said my good-byes, gave La'tian the metal box that controlled Go'lithum, then teleported Doc and I once more to the cave's entrance.

CHAPTER SIXTEEN

A Portal Home

We materialized outside the cave containing the sage.

"Sage of..." I started to yell.

"Yes, yes, there is no need to shout, I already knew you were coming. Come in, come in," he repeated sounding like a forgetful old man.

I walked into the cave with Doc beside me. As soon as we cleared the cave entrance, the interior came alive with light and activity. I looked behind me to see a grey shroud clouding the scenery beyond the cave, only making it possible to detect the outline of something in direct sunlight.

The interior was alive with moving apparatuses making sounds you would only hear in a cartoon. A small stream went through the cave which powered

Doctor Karmal's Machine

a water wheel. All the rest of the apparatuses were driven by this wheel. There were pulleys with ropes connected all over the place, driving gears that were doing a multitude of things. One was connected to a fan on the ceiling, another pumped water from the stream up a pipe just to pour a constant flow back into the stream. Another rope connected to a gear caused a feather fan that looked like a peacock's tail to fan some coals under a cauldron, keeping them red hot. Another one ran a kind of air pump and I could see a hose made out of some type of plant, wrapped with cloth here and there, attached to it. This hose was hissing from air pressure escaping. There were several other things that I couldn't even guess what they were for.

But what caught my eye the most was a very complex planet system made out of metal hanging over our heads. It had six planets slowly spinning around two fixed spheres in the middle, which I figured must be Surrea's two suns. Each of these planets had one or more spheres revolving around them, which I guessed were their moons.

I stood amazed at the complexity of his abode with everything being powered by the small water wheel. My spell was broken by the sage who was even more amazing than his residence.

He was barefoot and had webbed feet resembling a duck's, his legs compared to a horse's, his hands were human, except they were only four fingered. His arms looked like an ape's and his body was covered with clothing, so I had no idea what it looked like. But most amazing of all, his head and face looked just like a platypus, down to the duck-like bill.

He wore some type of head gear that resembled a sheiks turban.

"So, Sage of Zer'ical, how do I..."

"The Argom is the only thing in existence that can send you home."

"I really wish you would let me finish a question before you answer it," I said sarcastically. "Where is..."

"It is in the Cave of Hopelessness, in the Tal'kintion Mountains."

"Do you practice at doing that?"

"The coordinates of the cave are one thousand and eleven, by twenty-two hundred and one."

Well at least he answered that question before I could start it.

"The Argom is a huge instrument." He then described what sounded like a large pipe organ.

"The twentieth key from the left on the top row is the one you need to push. But I warn you, do not push any other keys. Each key does something different and there are one hundred and fifty-two of them. As far as I know, there is not anyone that knows what they all do, and the ones who have attempted to find out, all died trying."

I thanked the strange creature and walked out of his dwelling, since he said I could not teleport from within its confines.

"I guess it is just you and me, Doc." I began to teleport us to the coordinates he gave.

"What, you are just going to leave us behind?" A familiar voice asked from behind me. I spun to look at Glum, Glam, Omens, and Asmond.

"You didn't think we were going to let you be a jester to an empty court, did you?" Asmond asked. "And besides, who is going to save you when you get in trouble? Doc can only do so much."

We have some true friends here Doc. I am going to hate leaving them again.

That makes two of us Tom.

"Where to this time, Sire?" Omens asked, unknowingly interrupting our private conversation.

"The Cave of Hopelessness in the Tal'kintion Mountains and call me Sterling. I am no longer your King."

"You will always be my King," Glum said.

"Glumstron says for all," Glam added.

"To the Tal'kintion Mountains, the Argom awaits us." I commanded my loyal troops once again.

"You sure know how to choose an adventure. That cave didn't get its name for being just a joust," Glum stated as we prepared to leave the entrance to the unusual sage's dwelling.

We materialized in front of a set of caves along a cliff facing. There was a stairway cut into the rock going up to the second and third tiers.

"Each cave has a name, and each one has a reason for its name," Asmond stated.

I counted fifteen caves, six on the ground level, then four on the second level, and finally five on the top one. Since the one we wanted was called the Cave of Hopelessness, I could only imagine what the other fourteen names were.

Glum pulled out the Stone of Direction and tossed it into the air. It pointed at the stairs meaning the entrance we were looking for was one of the nine above us. After several tosses of the stone, we ended up standing in front of the cave we were seeking. I led the way with Doc just behind me, next came Asmond, then Glum, and last was Omens who had transformed into a smaller version of himself and took up the rear with Glam.

Asmond cast several light spells on an object each person carried, to light our way in the pitch-black darkness of the cave's interior. We marched into the Cave of Hopelessness, recklessly searching for adventure.

Since this would probably be the last time we traveled together, tension hung in the air. I felt like it was boy's night out, the day before I was to be married, and tomorrow my life would be completely different.

We marched on in silence, each one lost in their own private thoughts, private that is to everyone but Doc.

You know they don't want you to leave, they would all follow you to their deaths, if you wanted them to.

But there is a home, family, and friends back on earth. All we have here are friends, since I lost my family and home.

True, but friends like these are hard to find. Whatever you decide to do I will follow you.

We go back to our true home.

After we traveled a couple hundred feet from the entrance, the cave started to look like a manmade complex. Glum noticed me examining the workmanship.

Doctor Karmal's Machine

"Dwarven made, most dungeon complexes are. Or at least the ones still standing," he said smirking.

The farther we went, the more it looked like the hallways of a castle, than the tunnels of a cave. The only time our silence was broken was when Glum consulted the stone as to the direction of our goal. We marched deeper and deeper into the Cave of Hopelessness' depths, going down one hall then another. Through room after room, the place reminded me of my excursion through Horzule's Keep.

We came out into a room that looked like a pharaoh's burial chamber. There was no other apparent way out of the room, yet the stone pointed into it. Several caskets were scattered around the room and a stone tomb rested in the center, covered with a large stone slab.

We moved into the burial chamber and using the stone for guidance looked for what was apparently a hidden door. It pointed straight across the room, so we went toward the opposite wall.

"Mummies!" Glum yelled.

I turned to see what I would describe as the classic mummy moving toward us. Omens breathed on it but the fire from his breath had no effect on the undead creature as it continued its slow shuffle toward us.

"I have never encountered so many fire-resistant creatures in my life since I have met you Sire," he remarked sarcastically with a huge grin.

"Maybe magical fire will affect it." Asmond cast a fireball spell. Again the mummy walked through the blaze unaffected.

Tom, behind you, Doc warned.

I spun to see two more of the dead things shuffling toward us.

"Another blocks the door!" Glam shouted.

We were completely surrounded by the wrapped corpses. I jumped forward and rammed Sword into the one closest to me. Sword buried itself into the creature's chest without slowing it down a bit. I had to duck its slow swing, barely managing to withdraw Sword as I jumped back.

"How do you stop these things?"

"Normally fire, but they are being protected from it somehow," Glum answered.

"Glum, find the door while we keep them busy." I teleported behind one and swung down on its leg as hard as I could, cleaving clean through it. As soon as Sword passed through its leg, there was a colorful light that resembled a Fourth of July sparkler, and the leg fussed back together.

The mummy turned on me and attacked as I stood dumbfounded by my useless efforts to disable the thing. I easily dodged its attack and chopped through the arm, only to witness the same effect my blow had on its leg. Even before the appendage had a chance to drop off, it healed back into place before my eyes.

I was quickly running out of options and noticed nobody else was doing any better. I began to think they might be indestructible.

Well if I can't kill them, then I might as well contain them, I thought to myself. So, I cast a force field around the one in front of me, only to watch it pass right through the barrier like it wasn't even

Doctor Karmal's Machine

there.

"They're affected by cold!" Asmond shouted after he froze one solid with a freeze spell.

"The stone points to the tomb in the center of the room," Glum stated.

I cast a magical ice storm at the one in front of me, making sure to keep it away from my companions. The mummy was literally torn apart by the freezing hail that ripped through its body.

"Two down, two to go." I teleported to Glam's side and told him to go help Glum remove the tomb's cover, as Asmond took out another mummy.

The one in front of me quickly went down from another ice storm I cast in its direction once Glam was clear of the area. The last mummy had been destroyed.

Glum and Glam worked away at the heavy stone slab, but were unable to budge it. I came to their aid along with Omens. It still wouldn't move.

"Allow me," Asmond said with a confidence he rarely displayed.

We stood back while Asmond mumbled a few magical words and then brought his fist down on the stone cover. It shattered into small fragments, like it had been dropped from an enormous height.

We looked into the tomb and saw a ladder going down into the darkness. Instead of trusting the old decayed wood, I grabbed the dagger Asmond had cast a light spell on and dropped it down the shaft. The dagger hit the floor and lit the area below us, making it a simple task to teleport the group down. We materialized at the opening of a large cavern, the stone pointed into its dark confines.

I picked up the dagger, tossed it into the cavern, and watched it slide across the floor. It stopped about a hundred and fifty feet from us, throwing its light on a huge metallic object. The Argom had been found.

We cautiously covered the distance between it and us, watching the darkness, expecting something to jump out at us. To our surprise, nothing did.

I walked up to the Argom and carefully examined the three-level keyboard. The Sage of Zer'ical had said to push the twentieth key from the left on the top row. I counted the keys twice, to make sure I was pushing the proper key, heeding the warning he had given about pushing any others.

I looked at my friends standing behind me, intently watching my actions. And then finally, with a determination I had to find within me, pushed the key that would allow Doc and I to return to earth.

The Argom made a musical tone and a loud crackling noise came from out left. We all stared as the air swirled around and a portal that resembled a black hole in space appeared in our light. It looked similar to the portal I had gone through in the Hor'kuth Mountains the first time I had been on Surrea.

I looked back at the sad faces of my dear friends and then back to my way home.

"Ah, hell. My car was doing fifty when you brought me back to Surrea. I'm sure it's in a ditch somewhere. And in a month or two you will probably bring me back again because the universe needs saving. So, I might as well save you the trouble and just stay. What do you say, let's go take

Doctor Karmal's Machine

over a kingdom. I kind of fancy being called King Sterling."

I watched as four frowns turned into smiles.

"On one condition," Glum said.

"What's that?" I asked totally perplexed by his statement.

"You learn Surrean metaphor's. *I don't have the heart?* What is that supposed to mean?" He said with a loud laugh.

"It's a deal."

"And what is a car?" Omens said.

I laughed loudly and explained it was used like a horse and was mechanical.

We teleported out of the Cave of Hopelessness and the six of us had many more adventures together.

I did become a King again, but that is another story.

The End?

ABOUT THE AUTHOR

Born in Fresno, CA but raised in San Jose, CA, Neal Petersen's writing style was inspired by J. R. R. Tolkien. After being introduced to 'The Hobbit', required reading in the ninth grade, Petersen decided he wanted to try his hand at creating his own stories.

At an early age, Neal visited his brother and two sisters in the beautiful Ozarks. He attended college at MSU in Springfield, MO, where he still resides today.

Between the ages of nineteen to twenty-one, Petersen played many hours of Dungeons and Dragons. The game, along with Tolkien, inspired his stories.

He has written everything from short stories to novels, but his favorite has always been his creation, SURREA. The original story was written in 1990 and has taken twenty-seven years to get published. It's been a long, arduous journey.

Doc was the best dog Neal ever had. He still misses him.

Made in the USA
Coppell, TX
17 January 2022